"It happened without warning. Had the boilers blown, we might have heard the hiss of the steam before the plates blew, but in this case the resin-soaked wood was stacked too close to the overheated boilers and suddenly burst into flames.

"In ten seconds the boiler deck was a roaring furnace. This heat made the overtaxed boilers blow up. Burning wood was scattered over the rest of the boat and it became one huge torch.

"Men and women struggled and fought to get at the two yawls which were overside and ready to be lowered. I thought only of papa and mama, trapped below. I had to reach them. I rushed across the deck, but when I came to the stairwell, a gust of fire lashed out. I jumped back so quickly that I stumbled and fell.

"Strong hands lifted me to my feet and an arm went around my waist . . ."

THE DUNCAN DYNASTY

DOROTHY DANIELS

WARNER

PAPERBACK LIBRARY
NEW YORK

WARNER PAPERBACK LIBRARY EDITION
First Printing: March, 1973

Cover illustration by Walter Popp

*Warner Paperback Library is a division of Warner Books, Inc.,
315 Park Avenue South, New York, N.Y. 10010.*

One

I waited for Papa to seat me at one of the center tables in the dining salon of the *Orleana*, a new, resplendent Mississippi riverboat due in New Orleans in one more day.

It had not been a strenuous journey; the packet was the last word in luxury. My cabin was paneled in mahogany, with built-in dresser and bureau, a carved four poster and large windows through which I could watch the ever-changing pattern of the shore from St. Louis all the way to New Orleans.

Papa was putting on weight, but at forty-five was still a handsome man. As always, he was meticulously dressed, insisting that a morning frock coat was in order, especially on a grand riverboat.

Mama was a quiet woman. Not subdued, but preferring to let others do most of the talking. She was younger than Papa by six years and looked so young that we were often mistaken for sisters. We did look much alike. Mama was fair-skinned, believing too much sun was bad for the body. Her hair was a light brown, her eyes grayish-blue. She had a small, evenly shaped nose, an oval face and a well-formed mouth meant for smiling. I adored them both.

Papa, as usual, ordered a lavish breakfast and peered out of the dining salon windows while we waited for the first course to be served.

"We passed the *Prairie Queen* during the night, they tell me. Our captain is determined to reach the next port first, so he can pick up a large cargo and the mail. This rivalry between these packets is amazing."

"I do not like the speed they assume," Mama said. "It does seem to me it's dangerous."

"Too many of these boats have exploded," I commented. "Not that I believe this one will, but still they do keep the boilers terribly hot."

"They pour oil and resin on the wood for a hotter fire," Papa explained. "Well, it will be over this afternoon. One more docking before we reach New Orleans."

"I'll be most content when we finally arrive, Robert, but I do wish we had a house ready for us." Mama constantly worried about living in hotels.

"We'll have one within a week," Papa said confidently. "There's not a thing to worry about. I'll have my own business going promptly and I have every assurance I shall prosper. And I look forward to living in a warm climate. It should be quite a change. Besides, I have my cousin, Claude Duncan, to look up. Surely his advice will be beneficial."

"The idea of living in New Orleans fascinates me. I'll want to see everything," I said. "And if we can afford it, buy some new gowns. I understand they import them directly from Paris."

"No doubt," Papa said, "we can afford whatever you wish."

"Robert," Mama lowered her voice, "I'm much against you carrying all that money, even if it is in a money belt and out of sight. It's everything we have."

"And quite a lot too," Papa smiled. "Don't worry, it will be safe enough until I find the right bank. There have been a number of failures in New Orleans since the war and I didn't want to take a chance on forwarding our money to a bank I knew nothing about. Safer to carry it with you."

"You know best about that," Mama said.

Our first course of sliced peaches in yellow cream arrived. The head waiter followed up to make sure everything was in order.

"We're running four hours ahead of schedule," he

6

told us proudly. "We ought to break records this time. Captain Beardsley is determined to make this one of the fastest packets on the river."

I could feel the ship pulsating beneath my feet. From where I sat I could see the widening plumes of black smoke pouring from the feathered stacks, and it seemed to me they were putting on more and more pressure for speed. I began silently to pray we wouldn't be the fastest packet *under* the river.

Before breakfast was over, Mama was plainly frightened and even Papa seemed worried. I was making my first steamboat voyage, so the signs that bothered Mama and Papa meant little to me. The shaking of the ship, the huge columns of thick smoke, the laboring of the engine and the shouts of the firemen, were only part of everyday life on a packet so far as I was concerned.

I had read, of course, about the horrible disasters which had occurred along the river when boats blew up, caught fire and sank in minutes, or sometimes crashed against some strong snag in mid-river and promptly sank. There'd been a large loss of life on these packets, but I relied on the fact that they'd been sailing the Mississippi since the turn of the century and now, in 1885, they had certainly been improved upon and made safer.

After breakfast Mama and I took our daily constitutional along the deck, while Papa made his way to the boiler deck to have a look at the situation there.

"I did hope that we'd be settled in St. Louis for the rest of our lives," Mama said. "Your father is an ambitious man and St. Louis wasn't big enough for a merchant with his everlasting push."

"Oh Mama," I said, "it will be so different in New Orleans. So lively and full of fun. I'm looking forward to it."

"Well, a change is always good, especially for one as young as you, Jana, but I felt settled and I did not desire change. However, we shall make the best of it."

"They say there's theatre and opera, gay dances and balls. I'm sure we'll be happy."

"No doubt. And young men too, of which there seemed a dearth in St. Louis. At least the type I would approve of. I have heard they are quite the dandies. Much like that young man standing at the rail and looking at you in a way I used to delight in noticing when I was young."

I turned casually to see whom she meant, though I thought I knew. He hadn't said a word to us, but he seemed to make it a point to be on deck when we were. I judged him to be about thirty years old, a tall, slim man with black hair and dark brown eyes. He was not a handsome man, but he carried himself well and was possessed of a great deal of poise. I thought him rather rugged looking despite the fact that he was carefully and well dressed. His short jacket was a double breasted reefer in white, his trousers were gray and his black boots shiny and quite splendid. When I looked directly at him, he turned away quickly and pursed his lips in a soundless whistle meant to make him seem casual. I smiled to myself, but Papa's return made me forget him.

"You should see the way they're firing those boilers," he said. "There's a head of steam fit to blow them apart and, even worse, half the firemen are drunk. There's a stack of wood piled up almost against the boilers. The wood is dripping with resin. From where I stood, I could see the resin steaming from the heat. Frankly, I wish we'd put into some wharf so we could get off. Our captain is bound and determined to make history of this run, but it may be at considerable expense to his passengers and boat if those boilers ever let go."

"Please, Robert," Mama implored, "don't say such things. I'm distraught enough as it is. I do think I'd like to go to our cabin, if you don't mind."

"Of course," Papa said. "Coming, Jana?"

"I think I'll take the air a while longer," I said.

"Perhaps I'll join you later," Papa said. He led Mama

along the deck toward the staircase leading down to our cabins. For a moment, after they had gone, I thought the man in the white jacket would approach me, but he didn't. He continued to stand at the rail, now smoking a thin cheroot and apparently studying the muddy water that rushed under our keel.

It happened without warning. Had the boilers blown, we might have heard the hiss of the steam before the plates blew, but in this case the resin-soaked wood was stacked too close to the overheated boilers and suddenly burst into flames.

In ten seconds the boiler deck was a roaring furnace. This heat made the overtaxed boilers blow up. Burning wood was scattered over the rest of the boat and it became one huge torch.

Men and women struggled and fought to get at the two yawls which were overside and ready to be lowered. I thought only of Papa and Mama, trapped below. I had to reach them. I rushed across the deck, but when I came to the stairwell, a gust of fire lashed out. I jumped back so quickly that I stumbled and fell.

Strong hands lifted me to my feet and an arm went around my waist. "You can't do down there," my rescuer said. "Our only chance is to get off somehow."

It was the man in the white jacket. I was unable to speak. All of my thoughts were with my parents and already I knew there was no hope for them.

I saw the purser waving to me and indicating there was room in a yawl already jammed with passengers. The arm around my waist grew tighter.

"No," the man said. "The ropes by which the yawl will be lowered are already on fire."

As he spoke, one rope burned through. The prow of the yawl fell, three fourths of the people spilled out into the river. The boat, trying to make a sharp turn to head for the river bank, came to a dead stop. The hemp tiller ropes had also burned, making the boat unresponsive to the wheel.

I was unable to think. My father and mother were below decks where the fire raged out of control. The ship was beginning to list. It would surely go down in a few minutes. On deck the fight to survive was shameful. Had I not been held in the tight grasp of this benefactor, I would have been swept overside by the crush of people trying to get off.

The yawl on the other side of the boat managed to reach the water on a level keel before its ropes burned, but there the passengers, already overcrowding it, were assailed by many who had jumped from the deck to the yawl with the result that the small craft swamped in minutes and hope for those depending upon it for survival were gone.

The man at my side put his lips close to my ear so he might be heard above the din of screaming voices, falling debris, shouts of people in the water.

"Got to get off," he shouted. "I saw thirty barrels of gun powder aft, and the fire is sure to reach them. When it does. . . ."

"My father and mother. . . ." I cried out in anguish.

"You can't save them. Nobody can. Possibly they got off already. There was a hole blown in the side of the boat below decks. Come on! Can you swim?"

I nodded mutely. Tears were running down my face. I was too stunned to think. All I could do was obey this man. I discovered that I trusted him, for he seemed so strong and competent, and he showed no element of fear.

We reached the rail. Below us the water was crowded with people trying to stay afloat. So far no rescue vessel had appeared and it was obvious that many of the swimmers were going to die.

"One chance," my benefactor said. "Stay here! Don't move if you value your life."

He let go of me and dashed across the deck toward the yawl which had thrown out all its occupants by now, but which still hung by one hemp rope. The rope was smoking, but apparently had so far survived being severed by flames. My benefactor was about to remedy that. I saw him pick up a long stick of wood, burning fiercely at one end. He held this to the unburned rope until it caught fire, burned through, and the yawl fell into the water, keel first and, by plain good luck, didn't tip over even when people grasped it to climb aboard. There were so many that their frantic efforts from all sides of the boat kept it from tipping over.

He raced back to me, led me to the rail and showed me a length of rope tied to the rail. Because of the smoke and the fire, I hadn't seen him rig this lifesaving escape. He didn't have to instruct me. I knew by instinct what to do. I grasped the rope, went over the rail and slid down it directly into the boat.

Someone shoved it away from the packet. I looked up hoping that my benefactor was far enough down the rope to get aboard before it was too late. I didn't even see him. Someone found oars and the craft was now propelled at a rapid clip through the water. At the moment I thought it an extremely cruel thing to do, but those who tried to board us were ruthlessly pushed off, their hands clawing frantically at the sides of the yawl, being kicked free or pounded free by fists of the passengers. If another person came aboard, the yawl would founder and we'd all be drowned.

I felt the soft mud of the shore close around the prow. Everyone got off as quickly as possible. Two men had the courage and the good sense to push the boat away from shore, board it and row back to try and save some of the struggling people.

I wondered what had happened to the man who had saved me: I didn't wonder about my parents. I knew they must be dead. I was still too numbed by fear to mourn their loss at this moment. I began wandering about trying to help some of the injured and, at the same time, search for the man who had no doubt saved my life.

I found him, a few hundred yards away, frantically

11

looking for me. When we saw one another at a distance, he began running toward me and I toward him. We greeted one another with outflung arms and in a moment I was held tightly.

"I thought I'd lost you," he said. "There were so many in that yawl. . . ."

"And I thought you'd remained on board. I don't even know. . . ."

Further conversation was cut off by the roar of a terrific explosion aboard the packet. The gun powder had at last been touched off. Pieces of the craft sailed skyward, other parts fell into the water with great splashes. I guessed that many people were killed by the falling debris, there was so much of it.

I pressed my face hard against the man's jacket and I clung to him fiercely, as if I'd never let go. He led me away and I went with him, blindly, my eyes still fast shut against him. Finally we reached a dry spot and he eased me to the grass. He sat down beside me.

"I'm sorry about your mother and father," he said quietly. "You must realize nothing can be done for them. You have a right to mourn them, but not now. You have yourself to think about. Just as I have to think of myself."

"I know," I managed to say. "I'm so grateful for what you did. I'm sure I would not be alive had it not been for you."

"You'd have made it," he assured me. "Rest now. Lean against me. I think we're friends enough to be of comfort to one another. If you wish to cry, I'll understand that too."

"Later," I said. I leaned against him as he suggested. "Thank you again. I don't even know who you are."

"My name is David Brennan."

"I'll never forget you, Mr. Brennan. I am Jana Stewart."

"Jana? I never heard the name before. I like it. Yes . . . very much. Jana . . . it has a nice sound to it. Like music. I'm a musician."

"You play an instrument?" I asked. He was leading me into these kind of prosaic questions so I'd temporarily forget what had just happened.

"I play several instruments, but I'm actually a conductor. I was to appear in the New Orleans Opera House next week, but I'm not so sure now."

"I hope you'll be great," I said.

"Thank you. I'd better be. I lost everything I owned, except for a mighty small amount of money. That comes of carrying it with you. Only mine was in one of the suitcases and it's probably burned to a crisp by now."

"I'm sorry, Mr. Brennan."

"Oh, I'll make out. What of you?"

"I don't know." I was about to add that everything we had was also likely burned to a crisp, but I didn't want him worrying about me, nor did I wish him to share his meagre substance with me. He'd done enough.

"I have a relative . . . I can go to him," I added. "Please don't worry about me."

"It's my privilege to worry about ladies I helped save," he said with a smile. "We'd best do something about our clothes. We're soaking wet and we're lucky it's a warm day. I presume there will be some sort of transportation the rest of the way to the city. Shall we look for it now?"

"Yes," I said. "There's . . . nothing we can do here."

"I wish there was. I'm sorry, Jana. Dreadfully sorry."

I didn't reply because I was afraid if I did I might break down. Instead I let him take my hand and lead me to a dirt road down which we walked until we came to a group of stunned survivors. We were on a hillock overlooking the river now. All that we could see of the proud packet which had been trying to establish a speed record, was a mass of debris. The boat had disintegrated.

Mr. Brennan left me with two women who were obviously in need of comforting. I calmed them down and helped wring river water out of their voluminous dresses. Keeping active was good for me and Mr. Brennan seemed

13

to know that, for, when he returned, he put me to work caring for a three or four year-old girl whom no one had so far claimed.

I held her in my arms while Mr. Brennan told me they were sending another packet to pick us up. I would have preferred never to set foot on one again, but common sense told me there was no other good way to reach New Orleans.

By late afternoon I was dead tired from helping care for the injured. A packet finally arrived and a make-shift gangplank, twice as long as the average, was rigged up so we could get directly onto the boat.

When it steamed away, brushing aside the debris from the sunken packet, I felt the strength begin to drain out of me. Mr. Brennan sensed that I'd had all I could take. He'd managed to get a cabin assigned to me and he led me to it.

"Get undressed," he said, "and into bed. You need rest and warmth. When you're ready, call to me. I'll be right outside the door."

I nodded, again unable to speak. I managed to peel the sodden clothes off my body. I wrapped myself in large towels and got into bed. I finger-combed my hair, arranging it as best I could, before I called to Mr. Brennan.

He dragged a chair over beside the bed and sat down wearily. "I'm beginning to come apart," he confessed. "I have the next cabin, so all you have to do is rap on the wall and I'll be right over. Do you wish to talk, or would you rather try to sleep?"

"I couldn't sleep," I said. "I'd like to talk, if you can bear up."

"Don't concern yourself about me. Where did you come from?"

"St. Louis. My father was a merchant there. He had a large store and he planned to start another in New Orleans. Now . . . he and Mama . . . gone. It's hard to realize."

14

"I know. I'm lucky. I lost no one on board. You say you have a relative in New Orleans?"

"Very distant, but I'm sure he'll be able to help me."

"Of course he will, and before long you'll have everything straightened out. Will you remain in New Orleans?"

"I don't know. I haven't had time to think."

"I forgot to tell you . . . we'll put into a wharf before long, where good people have gathered clothing to replace what we were wearing. I'll see that you get a dress and . . . the other things."

"And what about you?"

"I'll do the best I can. I think I can save my clothes, but your dress . . . shoes . . . all the rest of it. I'm afraid. . . ."

"I know," I said. "I examined them a few minutes ago. They cannot be washed or repaired."

"At least we can soon remedy that situation."

"Do you know how many managed to get off?" I asked.

He shook his head. "No firm estimate, but they think about one third of us lived through it. Most were drowned."

"No word of . . . ?"

He cut me short. "None. All who were below decks went down with the remnants of the ship. In deep water. I doubt any attempt will be made to raise the hull."

"Then there's nothing for me but try to do the best I can in New Orleans."

"I hope you will permit me to be of whatever assistance I can," he said.

"You saved my life," I said. "I cannot be further in debt to you, Mr. Brennan. You've done more than enough."

"No, not half," he told me. "Not a fraction of what I'd like to do. This is certainly not the time to speak of it, but I have admired you for days."

I nodded and managed a smile. "I know."

"I hope I didn't offend you?"

"No, not in the least."

"I think you'd best try to rest now. Remember, I'm in the next cabin."

He arose, bent down to touch my cheek with his fingertips and to smile. "It's not easy, and tomorrow it won't be any easier. But you must stand up to it. We all must. I'll look in later. We won't reach the city until morning, so we've plenty of time."

"Thank you once again," I said, and I closed my eyes when a great weariness descended upon me. I heard him close the door and then I fell into a stuporous sleep brought on by a mixture of intense fatigue and a sorrow that drained me and left me weak and helpless.

Two

New Orleans was a bedlam of confusion and noise compared to St. Louis, but so much more colorful. Even in my profound sorrow, I realized the pace and the color here did a great deal to temper my sadness.

Mr. Brennan had provided me with a reasonably good outfit of clothes. They fitted well, but had seen better days so that I didn't present the kind of an appearance I'd hoped to for my first encounter with the city.

The streets were a wild tumult of drays, carriages, stately broughams containing stately ladies, buggies driven at furious speeds, men on horseback darting in and out of the traffic which seemed to have no order. It was every driver for himself.

Intermingled with this confusion were the pushcarts moving slowly along while the street vendors called out their wares. There'd been a great crowd at the dock to welcome the survivors, but all they did was stand around while the poor souls from the packet looked for friends or relatives.

Mr. Brennan had brought me to a quieter section of the wharf and we found a wooden bench on which to rest.

"I presume you will now find the relative you spoke of," he said.

"Yes, I must, for I certainly have to arrange my affairs and find something to do."

"Undoubtedly they will help you. I have several appointments I must keep. I wish I did not have to leave you."

"Mr. Brennan, you've done so much for me now that

I could ask no more of you under any circumstances. My wish is that you will lead your orchestra to a resounding success, and if I am here, I shall most certainly attend. And applaud the loudest, I hope."

"I can't very well see you again unless I know where you'll be."

"Frankly, I'm not sure myself. My relative is named Claude Duncan. Where he lives or what he does, I have no idea. Perhaps it would be better if I found you."

"Then you do wish to see me again, Jana?"

"How could I wish otherwise, after what you did for me? Of course I want to see you again."

"Ah—good! I am going to try for the position of conductor of the opera and I shall be at the French Opera House. You will be able to find out there exactly where I am located."

I arose and extended my hand. "I know you have business and you must go. Please do not worry about me. I'm sure I shall be well taken care of until everything is settled."

He took my hand between both of his. "I grieve for your parents," he said. "I pray that you will soon get over your loss, though I know it will not be easy. I shall look forward to seeing you again, as soon as possible."

"Thank you . . . David," I used his first name. "Please go now."

He smiled, turned and walked away. I waited until he was out of sight, swallowed up by the crowd on the wharf. Only then I began to walk toward a group of people assembled under a crude sign indicating that this was where survivors without money or relatives would be cared for.

A portly, perspiring man took my name down and told me I would have to see the Judge of the Probate Court at once because I had neither money nor a place to stay. He gave me a few coins, strange ones to me, called picayunes. He also gave me directions to the building where I would find the judge.

18

I made my way across the crowded streets, dodging the variety of vehicles and finding myself slightly bewildered by all the commotion. I crossed a square where groups of women sat about, small negro children were jigging for coins, vendors were selling a concoction of shaved ice covered with a sickeningly sweet syrup. I spent some of my picayunes on a cup of this, but found it all but tasteless, though cooling to the mouth.

I, who had never known what it was like to be alone and completely dependent upon myself, found the experience anything but exhilarating. I was frightened and uncertain of myself with my great sorrow lurking at the back of my mind—sorrow I'd not yet found the time, nor the opportunity to dwell upon. I hadn't even found the time to miss Mama and Papa.

I discovered that my destination was a red brick, two-story building in which I had to ask directions to Judge Lamonthe's office. There I found others in my position, also gathered. All of them grieving, or scared to death by being so suddenly thrown upon a city for support, having lost everything they owned.

I waited patiently. There wasn't anything else for me to do. I did think of trying to find Claude Duncan, but knowing nothing about him, or his family, I was reluctant to throw myself upon his mercy. First I would see if there was any way I might make a living here and remain independent.

Finally I was ushered into a drab-looking office. Behind a long desk sat a heavily jowled man with thinning hair and the unmistakable aroma of recently imbibed whiskey about him.

"Name please," he said gruffly.

I gave it and the pertinent facts about my position. He made his notes, leaned back and frowned heavily.

"In the consideration of this court you are an orphan, homeless, without funds, or work, or friends. Am I correct, Miss Stewart?"

"Yes indeed, you are, sir," I replied.

19

"Are you trained in any sort of work?"

"No sir. I left finishing school eight months ago and I have not been employed since."

"Well, don't look to me to get you work, Miss. I'm in no position to render such a service. However, you must find work or you will be declared indigent and you will be farmed out to work at anything that turns up. It will likely be field work."

I must have looked as uncomprehending as I felt.

"You lost your parents," he went on. "Did they not leave you anything?"

"Papa sold all he owned in St. Louis and he was carrying all of his money on him when the ship blew up."

"Then don't anticipate finding the money because anybody on that ship when the gun powder went off was blown to smithereens. What will you do for the night?"

"I don't know, sir."

"In my opinion I should declare you an indigent now. I think you will have to spend the night locked up. Can't have a young girl roaming about our streets all night."

"Do you mean, sir, that I shall be imprisoned?" I asked, finding that hard to believe.

"That's what I mean. It's against the law in New Orleans to be without money, friends, a job, a place to stay, or . . . relatives."

"Just one moment. . . ." I tried to interrupt him.

"Now, young lady, there'll be no arguing this point. You are to be pitied, I'm sure, but this court cannot operate on pity and there are no provisions to care for such as you. Therefore, you will go to jail until we finally dispose of your case."

"A relative," I cried out. "Sir, I do have a relative. Or rather, my father had one. A cousin whom he was going to contact after he settled down here with Mama and me. Surely you will allow me to find this relative."

"Your father's cousin. That's distant all right. I don't know. I think we should lock you up. For your own good, mind you."

"The name of my relative is Claude Duncan, sir."

The bushy eyebrows shot upwards, the jaw dropped and remained slack until the judge recovered his composure. He braced his hands on the arms of his chair as if to get up abruptly, but he sank back again instead.

"Claude Duncan?" he said. "You do mean Claude Duncan?"

"Why yes. That's the name Papa spoke."

"You have never met him?"

"No, sir. I never even heard of him until we were ready to make this journey."

"Claude Duncan," he said, and slapped his fat thigh as if in great amusement.

"Is there something wrong with Mr. Duncan?" I asked apprehensively. He was my last resort.

Judge Lamonthe emitted a roar of mirth, arose, seized my arm, half lifted me from my chair and led me to one of the windows in his office. It overlooked the large, sprawling and busy city square.

"See there!" He pointed to a large and imposing theatre. "Our best theatre. And there . . . to your right . . . the opera house, modeled after one in Vienna. The large hotel . . . the smaller one . . . that row of beautiful houses . . . all of that—every part of it is owned by Claude Duncan, and you have not seen a fraction of his worth here in the city. There is also his plantation, which is miles square. I don't know just how many. He employs about two thousand people and keeps a great plantation house of forty and more rooms. If he snapped his fingers, I could lose my position and everything else I have accumulated. He is a man to have as a friend, and then you will be among the lucky. If he is your enemy, prepare for the worst, for you cannot win against a man such as he. That is your father's cousin."

I went back to my chair, somewhat breathless at being even a remote relative of this man. The judge sat down too and hastily wrote a note. He picked up a small brass bell, rang it and a clerk responded at once. The judge gave him orders to see that the note reached Claude Duncan at once.

"And in person," he said. "This is important. Also, hurry. We do not wish to have Mr. Duncan regard us as laggards, eh?"

"No, sir," the clerk replied with emphasis. "I'll ride out there at once."

The judge gave a snort of exasperation aimed at himself. "To think I might have locked you up as a pauper. Had I done so and Claude Duncan learned of it . . . off goes my head. I pray that you will forgive my rudeness, but in my position a man has a duty to perform and he must not be swayed by pity."

"I quite understand, sir," I told him. I would have forgiven anything at this moment, for I felt as if a mighty weight had been lifted from me.

"You will, no doubt, go to Duncan Empire . . . that is what we call his plantation and his mansion . . . to live. It is the grandest place in New Orleans, probably in all of Louisiana. Mr. Duncan is not niggardly when it comes to providing himself with those things he enjoys."

"Mr. Duncan is a married man, I presume?"

"Oh yes . . . married, yes. His wife is Celina, a grand and important woman who knows the meaning of power. They have one child, a son, who is now . . . let me see . . . twenty-four years old. And Celina's sister lives there. A woman named Augusta Flores, a Creole, and proud as they come."

"I shall look forward to meeting them," I said with enthusiasm.

"My child, I cannot say what I think, so again, forgive me. It is not well to comment on these people, for they have great power that goes with great wealth. Their friends are numberless. They give elegant soirées, dinners and dances. Sometimes they use the ballroom in their hotel for these affairs, though in my estimation, their house is almost as big as the hotel. You will have much to learn and get used to."

I was by now vaguely suspicious of the judge's attitude toward the Duncans and I began to entertain some doubts about them myself. Naturally I could not comment and, it appeared, the judge was afraid to.

His chief clerk tapped on the door, opened it and peered in inquisitively. "Pardon, your honor, but there are many others waiting. . . ."

"Let them wait," the judge said. "We are honored to have with us a relative of Claude Duncan. The others will have to be patient."

The clerk's smile was ingratiating, as if I were the head of the Duncan clan. "I'm sorry to have intruded," he said. "I shall have the others wait."

I tried to tell the judge I could wait elsewhere, but he would have none of that. I was a Duncan and I deserved his uninterrupted attention. Almost an hour and a half went by before I heard rapid, firm footsteps cross the outer office, the door was thrown wide and a man of about Papa's age marched in. He didn't simply walk, he strode as if in time to band music. He was tall, thin and sharp-faced, with sparse, graying hair and pale blue eyes. They were the most arrogant eyes I had ever seen, boring into mine. Perhaps there was a faint resemblance between him and Papa, but one would have to look closely to detect it. Papa had been handsome. Mr. Claude Duncan was definitely not, with his long nose, thin slit of a mouth and deep-set eyes. His dress was a good portrayal of his wealth and standing, for he wore striped trousers tucked into hand-made boots, a colorfully pink and blue shirt with a bright yellow weskit and, over all this, a blue, formal coat.

"It is a great honor. . . ." the judge began.

"This is she?" Claude Duncan motioned me to stand up. "Robert's girl, eh? What are you doing here, and why was I not notified you were coming?"

"My papa and mama," I said, "were killed in the riverboat explosion. I was saved. That is why I'm here, in the courtroom. All I owned, clothes, everything, was destroyed by the fire and explosion. Nothing of Papa's or Mama's is left. Everything he owned was destroyed as well. In short, sir, I am a pauper without work or funds, and not trained to earn my own way."

"If you're looking for sympathy, you get none from me. What is your name?"

"Jana Stewart, sir."

"How long have they kept you in this . . . this . . . pig-sty?"

"Not long," I said, startled and annoyed by his arrogance. The judge had been kind to me, once he discovered who I was.

"I should have been informed immediately. You say you have nothing, which means you stand in the only possessions you have, your clothing. Very well. Come with me."

He held a riding crop and he slapped his booted leg with it to create a sharp crack of sound as he strode out of the office without waiting for me. I took time to thank the judge and then I ran after Mr. Duncan, feeling as abject about it as the judge must be feeling right now.

Outside, I saw a black carriage drawn by two of the loveliest and best groomed black stallions I'd ever seen. Before I reached it, Mr. Duncan was seated and slapping the reins for the team to get going. I had to get aboard as the carriage began moving. He began talking before I settled myself beside him.

"Your father was as poor as you are now, I suppose," he said. "I haven't seen him in years or heard a word from him."

"My father was a prosperous merchant in St. Louis," I said indignantly. "We were far from poor. But he sold everything he had to come here and settle down. The wealth he had accumulated sank with him and the ship, or was blown to bits. I do not know which, but I am told there isn't the slightest use in trying to find . . . anything."

"You're taking it well, seeing it only happened a matter of hours ago."

"The tears," I said, "will come later."

"Well said. Do you have any spirit, my lass, eh?"

"I don't know what you mean by spirit," I said half angrily. I had no intention of allowing this man to dominate me as he very likely did everyone else.

He pulled up the team sharply, so that I was jolted forward. He twisted around in his seat. "I asked you a question and you did not see fit to give me the direct answer it deserved. I want answers to my questions."

He drew back his arm and slapped me across the face very hard. I was too aghast to do more than cry out. He slapped me again and then a third time. By then I was over my surprise and chagrin and my temper boiled. I struck back at him, slapping him as hard as I could across the mouth. Then I shrank back in the anticipation of being given a solid drumming. Instead he threw back his head and laughed.

"Yes, you have it, by heaven. You've spirit! There's nothing I admire more. Indeed, it is a rare asset. We shall do fine, my lass. And I may add, you swing a hefty blow, for a girl such as you."

I was still raging. "I am not given to the kind of temper I have just displayed unless I am forced into it. I know you are a wealthy and a powerful man, but to me that means little or nothing. I am obliged to you, but that does not mean I shall allow myself to be trampled on."

"My dear, I just told you my admiration is now boundless. I wished to discover for myself if you were wishy-washy as so many girls are these days. However, I also do not believe in charity, not even for those close to me by blood. And especially for those as remote as you. Here and now I give you a choice. You will be welcome at my home, but you will work for everything granted you. That, or you may get out here and walk back to the city where you will present yourself to the judge and tell him I will have nothing to do with your welfare. After which he will lock you up until he finds someone weak enough to pity you and give you work. I do not believe in pity."

"At least, sir, you are frank about it. I will agree to your terms and I will gladly work for my found. I shall be grateful, but please do not expect me to respect and admire you. I admire people who are like my father, not such as you, sir."

"It is agreed then," he said. He picked up the reins. "You are a winsome lass. More than that, you're attractive. Indeed you are, my dear girl. Something may come of this after all. We shall see."

I did not ask him what he meant by that, because I was convinced he wouldn't have answered me anyway. During the remainder of the drive of almost an hour's time, he asked me questions about the tragedy and while he listened attentively and with interest, he never once betrayed the slightest amount of concern. As he had so baldly stated, he did not admire pity in anyone, least of all in himself, apparently.

He cast a sidelong look my way. "I have a son, twenty-four years old. How old are you?"

"Twenty, sir."

"My son is irresponsible, lazy, wicked, treacherous and incompetent. You will like him."

I couldn't contain the laugh that escaped me for the way he described his son. He grinned at me and, for an instant or two, we were conspirators in judging the poor qualities of his son.

"He was married," he explained, "but his wife couldn't stand him and went off somewhere. Not that he cares. I doubt he even misses her. Who told you about my family?"

"The judge, sir."

"I expected it might be he. What else did he say about my people?"

I had no desire to get the judge into trouble, so I chose my words carefully. "He said your wife is an aristocrat, a beautiful woman."

"She is, indeed. What else?"

"Well, he stated that her sister lives with you."

26

"Did he say anything about Laverne?"

"It is the first time I heard the name mentioned, Mr. Duncan."

"He is a lifelong friend of mine and he also knew your father—and your mother. I think he used to be in love with her many years ago. I demand that you be pleasant to him."

"I know of no reason why I should not be pleasant to all your family, sir."

"Wait until you meet them," he chuckled. "There's also Odette. She has been my housekeeper and my father's housekeeper. She seems to be ageless and she runs the house the same way I run the plantation, without nonsense."

"I can respect that too," I told him.

He nodded briefly and suddenly seemed reluctant to talk more. I withdrew into a leisurely examination of the landscape—the little cabins and their small vegetable gardens, the countless barns and stables, the spring houses and red-painted sheds. The road was rutted so deeply that it was unnecessary to direct the horses. They simply inserted the wheels in the ruts and the direction took care of itself.

To my right was open farm land, plantation property, which, I learned later, belonged to Mr. Duncan. All of it. His empire ran for miles. To the left of the road we had traveled behind the protection of rows of tall trees, with heavy foliage. These suddenly stopped. I discovered we were close to the Mississippi. Here it was so gentle and quiet that it could not be heard and no boats were presently near us, so my surprise was complete when we came upon the river.

My next surprise took place when I first saw the grove of trees in the distance. It looked to me like an oasis in a desert of prairie, farm and pasture land. Slowly as we approached, the mansion seemed to grow out of the air. It was so cleverly placed amidst that group of trees that it was often hidden when the road made a turn this way

27

or that. The closer we got, the more the mansion remained in view and soon I had a very good look at it.

I saw a two-story building, consisting of a main structure with a wide, rambling porch topped by a green shingled roof held up by ten massive white pillars. The main house had a wing at each end. One of these rose to three stories in height. I learned the third floor was for the use of the servants.

The number of chimneys gave an indication to the number of rooms. The building was not new, but it showed no signs of weathering. All around it was closely cropped lawn and I could see at least four men busy at work tending to it and the shrubs and the flower gardens.

"How do you like it?" Mr. Duncan asked.

"Most imposing," I said.

"That's how I meant it to be. People like to be impressed, especially by those who have the wealth to do it well."

We turned down a lane and presently pulled up before the entrance, as dominating as the house itself. The double doors extended all the way to the balcony overhang. Yet they could be opened as easily as a regulation-sized door, a fact I never quite got used to and I invariably prepared myself to use a great deal of strength to get the massive door open.

When it admitted me for the first time it was opened by Odette, the housekeeper. Her age was impossible to guess, though I never did consider her younger than sixty-five. She was short, wizened, her face as wrinkled as mountain crags. She wore brown, always. A light brown shirtwaist, a dark brown skirt over which she tied a white apron. I never came to see the slightest marks of soil on any of the aprons and I judged she must change them several times a day.

"This," Mr. Duncan said, "is the daughter of my cousin Robert who, with his wife, went down with the packet. Miss Jana Stewart will live with us. She will be assigned work later, when we discover what she can do. For now, I wish you to take her to one of the spare rooms."

"Guest rooms, sir, or servant's quarters?"

"Guest room for the time being at least. I should judge her to be about the same size as Marie. Wouldn't you, Odette?"

"*Oui*, perhaps a bit scrawnier." Odette's cold eyes surveyed me critically.

"You will turn over to her every stitch of clothing Marie left behind. All of it, without exception."

"*Oui, M'sieur.*"

"When you have rested," he told me, "my wife will wish to see you. That's all."

"Come," Odette said curtly.

I followed her up the wide, curving staircase and I had a glimpse of what this mansion must be like. The entrance hall was wide and long, lighted by five great chandeliers sparkling in the light of the late afternoon sun that entered a large window located halfway up the staircase, where it curved so gracefully.

The walls were papered with hunting scenes. The stairs were covered with deep carpeting. The second floor landing hall appeared to occupy the length of the main house and the bedrooms were on both wings. I was led along the one to my right. All the way down the corridor to the last room.

It proved to be small, not much above that which a servant was expected to use. The furniture consisted of an iron bed, painted white, a plain dresser of unbleached wood, a somewhat wavy mirror above it and a single stuffed chair. There was, however, a private bathroom.

I cared little for the comforts. I waited until Odette closed the door behind me and then I flung myself across the bed and the tears which I'd successfully blocked all day long, now came copiously.

I wasn't ashamed of them.

Three

I must have dozed finally, because when the heavy pounding on my door brought me sitting up, I was confused as to exactly where I was. Sad memory returned with a savage rush. I felt that my face was swollen and my eyes must be reddened, but there was no denying whoever all but broke the door down.

It was suddenly flung wide and a tall, muscular looking man strode in imperiously. He wore a tweed spring jacket, breeches tucked into brown leather boots, a ruffled shirt and a flowing black tie. He was a striking looking man without being handsome. His thick black hair was long, his temples adorned by heavy sideburns. His features were strong, except for the eyes. They were a pale blue and looked to me like ice. I knew he must be Walter Duncan.

"Crying," he said callously, "is for babies. Papa said you were beautiful. I suppose you are when you haven't been weeping. Come downstairs. Mama wishes to see you at once."

"As promptly as I can," I said.

"Don't keep her waiting. She hates that. But I'd advise you to wash your face first. Mama hates a weeping female as much as I do. Get on with it, girl. Don't stand there." At the door he looked back. "I'm Walter," he added.

I fled to the bathroom and splashed my face generously. I dried it, did my best to make my less-than-stylish dress somewhat presentable. I tried to fix my hair, but I had neither comb nor brush, so I could do little with it. When I walked into the bedroom, Walter had gone, but in his place stood a woman who smiled at me and extended both

31

hands. This, I guessed, could not be Mrs. Duncan, so it must be her sister.

"My dear child, how lovely you are. I grieve with you over the loss of your mama and papa. I know they must have been fine people."

"Thank you," I said.

"Oh—I haven't told you who I am. My name is Augusta Flores. I am Mrs. Duncan's sister."

I gave a startled gasp. "Mrs. Duncan sent for me. I must go. . . ."

"Fiddlesticks! Let her wait. Tell her I insisted you talk to me first. She's afraid of me."

"Are you sure of that?" I asked, trying to fall in with her light mood because I enjoyed it.

"Indeed she is. You see, I'm younger than she is, and she's afraid I'll tell that secret and reveal how old she really is. She's vain and self-centered, and she couldn't stand for her true age to be revealed. That is my hold on her."

I hadn't seen Mrs. Duncan yet, but Augusta Flores was completely gray, her skin somewhat mottled and wrinkled, though she didn't look like an old lady, nor in any way act like one.

"I still believe I'd best go down," I said.

"Yes, I suppose so. A word of warning. Not about her. Heaven knows you'll learn to handle yourself as far as my beloved sister goes. I wish to warn you about Walter. He's handsome and charming and completely rotten. You are more than pretty, so he'll be howling after you."

"Thank you for the warning," I said. "Please excuse me now."

I hurried downstairs. I wasn't sure where I was supposed to go, but I assumed it would be the drawing room. I hadn't entered it before, so when I did walk in, I came to a dead stop in total admiration.

It occupied two thirds of the main house. Its ceiling was high, its expanse would allow a hundred couples to dance comfortably. The tall windows were curtained and draped in deep burgundy, the same color as the five carpets precisely laid to cover much of the floor space. The furniture was unmatched, but of the highest possible quality. I suspected most of it had been imported. The predominating color was gold. The walls were papered in that rich shade and it went well with the burgundy of the drapes and carpets. Furniture was massive, almost all of the chairs and sofas deeply padded. Unlike most drawing rooms, it was not cluttered with the usual bric-à-brac, but very plain with little adornment. If Mrs. Duncan was responsible for the interior of this house, I admired her fine taste.

But my concern was with her and not the appointments. She sat in a tall backed chair, her hands resting lightly on the arms of it. She wore a gown of pale blue china silk in the latest style, smooth over the hips, the skirt long and bell-shaped. It was modestly high at the neck, with a large bow of tulle.

As I drew closer, I could see why she would hate to have her sister relate the secret that she was the oldest, because Mrs. Duncan looked fifteen years younger than Augusta Flores. Her skin was unwrinkled and she possessed a haughty beauty. Her hair was flaxen, kept that way, I suspected, with a dye. If she had not been so austere and severe looking, she would have been a hauntingly beautiful woman.

As I approached, walking the entire length of the long room, she didn't move or comment. She simply looked at me quite casually until I had a feeling she would not have objected if I knelt before her and perhaps kissed the hem of her gown.

"Can you serve as my secretary?" she asked. There was no word of greeting nor commiseration for my recent loss.

"I believe I might, madam."

"What is your training, if any?"

"I graduated from the Faulker Finishing School this year."

"Ah yes. Do you speak French?"

"*Oui, Madame,* though not fluently."

"You should, you know."

"I speak Italian and Spanish as well, and I can read, write and speak in German."

"Well, we have a linguist, it appears. Do you write a legible hand?"

"Yes, quite legible. I received the highest grades in penmanship."

"That is, at least, an asset. What delayed you?"

"Your sister introduced herself. I could not offend her by walking away."

"You will from now on. She is a meddler. Breakfast is at eight, dinner at one, and supper at seven. Let me see, you will not dine with the servants, of course, for you are a blood relative. Yet not close enough to be permitted to the family table. You shall be sent a tray and you may dine in your room. For the present."

"Thank you, Mrs. Duncan," I said, as pleasantly as I could manage.

"Tomorrow you will report to me. I will see how good you are at secretarial work. Do you ride?"

"Yes, madam."

"You will accompany my son on some of his morning rides. None of us care to, and he enjoys company. You may take possession of all of his wife's clothing. Fortunately I'm sure they will fit."

"But what if she returns?" I asked.

"She will not. If by some chance she does, she won't be allowed in this house again. That's all."

I turned and took a few steps before I turned back to face her. "Thank you," I said dutifully.

"That's better," she said. Just as I suspected, she'd been expecting that homage, waiting for it. I wondered how long I could manage to put up with this strange household. At the moment I had no choice, so I would make the best of it.

It was, by now, almost dark as coolness swept away the

34

heat of this mid-summer day. I went to my room and looked out of the window. In the distance I could see what seemed to be a small city consisting of houses, all of the same kind. Perhaps identical, though I couldn't tell that from this distance. As I watched, I saw the first of the file of field workers returning home. They marched in a long line. They were all black and, of course, they'd once been slaves. Many of them, at least. They'd put in a long day at field work. I wondered, idly, if things had changed much for them. I knew they were being paid. The law required that, but they still worked long and hard. I raised a window to confirm the fact that they were singing. It was soft, melodious and sad. I pulled down the window quickly. What I didn't need at the moment was a song of sadness.

I wondered when I would have access to the cast-off, or leftover clothing from Walter's missing wife. At least I had a closet to store the dresses in. I opened the door to determine its size. It was large, and crammed with an assortment of extremely lovely and expensive clothes. While I'd been downstairs, someone had transferred Marie's garments to my room. This house was efficiently handled, if coldly.

I had to light the oil lamps and there were sufficient in number to give me all the light I required. I removed some of the clothes to examine them and tried on one pale blue dress of fine silk. It fit as if it had been made for me.

I looked in the bureau drawers and discovered they too had been filled with underthings, two corsets, fine hosiery. An upper drawer held combs, brushes, a chamois cloth and a small tin of rice powder. There were jars of skin cream, used, but fresh. I discovered bottles of imported colognes, ribbons in a wild assortment of colors. Scarves, shawls, cloaks, so many things I didn't have time to examine them all.

This morning I'd been destitute, clad only in a dress soaked by muddy river water and torn in several places. Now it was the evening of the day after and I had a surfeit of fine gowns and accessories. I supposed in a way I was fortunate. I wondered what had happened to Marie and what she'd been like. I did approve of her choice of clothing.

I knew without doubt that I'd be expected to rise early and be prepared for whatever orders I would be given. These had been the most trying two days of my life and I was on the point of exhaustion and more tears, so the prospect of bed was most inviting.

I opened the door in answer to a timid knock and found a pretty girl in a maid's uniform standing there with a tray in her hands. It seemed almost too heavy for this fragile girl and I quickly relieved her of it.

"Thank you, mum," she said, with a heavy Irish accent. I didn't know it then, but New Orleans had a large colony of Irish. " 'Twas near ready to drop, it was."

"Come in," I said.

"Well mum, this is a strict household as you'll well find out for yourself. It ain't right. . . ."

"As I understand it, I'm going to be as much employed in this household as you are. Now don't stand there. Come in."

She all but skipped into the room, looking highly pleased at the invitation.

"My name is Coleen, mum."

"I'm Jana Stewart and I'll be working as Mrs. Duncan's secretary."

"And heaven help you, mum," she said fervently.

"Why do you say that?"

"She's a mean one to work for, that she is. You might say she's an exacting woman." Coleen sighed deeply. "By heaven, that's sure the right word for her."

I removed the cloth from the tray and discovered a full meal, well cooked and well served. There was a floating island pudding which I liked, but I thought Coleen did too, so I gave it to her and she sat on the edge of the bed happily devouring it while we became good friends. I thought I needed one in this household.

36

"The master," she confided, "is a proud man. The rudest I've ever met and no doubt about it. To him the name Duncan means as much as the whole blessed world. I never heard of a man so disappointed when Walter's wife bore no sons. One thing he cannot stand is to have the name die. But it will when he does, and Walter comes into all of this. He will squander it surely as the existence of sin. He will, mum."

"What sort of man is Walter? I don't want to pry, but if I am to live here, I'd best be told about the people I will likely serve."

"They'll send me back to the Channel if they ever find out I told you, mum."

"The Channel?" I asked without understanding.

"It's the Irish Channel . . . where all the Irish in New Orleans live, and there's no tougher place in this or any other country, including Dublin. I don't want to go back there."

"Be assured," I told her, "that I will say nothing."

"Well, mum, he's no man I'd look at more than once, though I say he's not ugly, except where his nature is concerned. Sometimes I think the man is daft because of the things he does. But all I can say about him is that he's mean. He gambles like a fool and he drinks like a fish. But when he wants to, he can be as haughty as his ma and as tough as his pa. Once he was after me and I told him if he laid a hand on me I'd go back to the Channel and tell the boys. They'd come here after him and he knew it, so I ain't been bothered by him since. I think he's half mad since his wife up and left."

"He's the man I'm supposed to go riding with," I said with a shake of my head.

"Carry a quirt, mum, and use it if you have to. He ain't much of a one to stand up to those who sass him back. And are armed with a club."

"Did his wife leave him because she couldn't stand his ways?"

"Mainly so, I'd say. She was a pretty thing, but she

37

didn't have much spunk and she couldn't bear children. Leastwise they blamed it on her. She left sudden and she never came back. The old man is about to have her declared legally dead. He can do it, even if she hasn't been gone so long that enough time has passed to make it legal."

"I expect he'll get married again, in due time," I said.

"Who'd have the like of him? All New Orleans knows what he is. If he wasn't Claude Duncan's son, he'd have been challenged to a duel long ago and killed."

"Oh, but the money," I reminded her. "Rich men can always find wives."

Coleen started to say something, then apparently changed her mind. She spooned up the traces of pudding left on her plate, arose and prepared to take the tray away.

"I'd not close your eyes when Mr. Laverne Cavet is about either. He likes a pretty face and a well-shaped ankle too."

"Mr. Duncan did mention him as a friend."

"He's all of that, mum. He comes here often. Lives in a flat on Bourbon Street, but he's at home here too and he gives orders like the master. Expects them to be obeyed as well. He's getting on, but still, keep at least one eye open."

"What of Odette?" I asked, thinking to learn about all of these people while I had the chance.

"If I ever ask the help of the Irish Channel, it will be against her. She will be jealous of you because you are young. Watch out for her."

I gave Coleen a parting hug before she picked up the tray. "You've certainly braced me for trouble," I said. "Thank you. I think I can face these people with more confidence now."

I was again on the verge of exhaustion as I closed my door and prepared to retire early. I was pleased that I had not been invited to the family supper table, because then they'd never let me go. I preferred to be on my own.

I discarded all of the clothes donated to me. I laid out those articles of Marie's wardrobe that I would wear next day and put on one of her night dresses.

By nine I was in bed with the lamps out. The house was quiet, the room dark, and through this calm came the awful memory of the sinking of the packet and the deaths of my father and mother. I quieted my sobs by thinking about David Brennan and what he must be doing at the moment. He'd been so kind and thoughtful, besides actually saving my life, that I respected and admired him even after such a short acquaintance. I prayed that he would soon be leading the orchestra at the opera and making a name for himself and, eventually, become famous. I doubted I'd ever see him again. As of tonight it did seem to me that neither Claude Duncan nor his wife were going to permit me much freedom, let alone provide the means for me to travel to New Orleans when I wished.

My life from now on was going to be radically changed. I'd be a remote member of this family, and employed to pay for my board and keep. I doubted there would be any financial arrangement made, which would not make it any easier for me to eventually break away, as I already *had* made up my mind to do. One day soon I'd speak to Mr. Duncan about some cash payment for my services, but at the moment I was far too dependent on him to raise the issue. If he turned me out, I'd soon find myself facing the judge again and this time I might wind up in jail, or farmed out to someone where the work would be much more exacting. So I intended to make the best I could of the situation and bide my time.

Four

In the morning I began to discover what was expected of me. Because I'd retired very early, I was up, dressed and ready for the day when Odette knocked, a virtual hammering she must have employed because she believed I must still be abed. I opened the door and stood before it blocking any attempt on her part to enter.

"The help has already had breakfast," she said. "You will have yours in the kitchen, and no back talk about it. There's nothing wrong in eating there when you are not compelled to share the table with servants."

I said, "Madam, I have never indicated I disliked sharing my table with anyone. It was Mrs. Duncan's idea, not mine."

"Well, don't tarry then. Mistress wants you at her side as soon as you finish, so come at once."

I ate my breakfast with only a cheerful, brown-skinned cook from Jamaica as company. She told me her name was Silviana and that she was the best cook in the world, an opinion I soon found myself sharing with her.

Before I was half finished, Odette bustled into the kitchen to hurry me along. I left part of my breakfast and trailed behind her to the upstairs again. There she tapped on one of the doors, opened it and let me pass by her into Celina Duncan's parlor and then her bed chamber.

It was large and airy, though drapes were closed, curtains pulled and even the shutters tightly closed. As a result the room was so dark that Mrs. Duncan had lit three large lamps, though it was bright and sunny outside.

On the bed before her was a bedtable on which lay a

substantial pile of what seemed to be letters. Celina indicated them.

"I have been lax in my correspondence and I shall now leave it to you. I have made notes on each letter indicating how I wish them answered. Your ingenuity will no doubt provide very good and effective replies. When you have finished this chore, I shall find other things for you to do."

The "other things" she referred to consisted of cutting flowers, arranging them, reading to her, darkening the room for her afternoon nap, delivering orders to the cook and to Odette, preparing shopping lists of every need save those connected with the kitchen.

For three days I worked from early morning until Celina decided to retire, and each night I felt as exhausted as I had the night after the tragedy. So far, Claude Duncan had stayed away from me and Walter seemed to have spent the last three days in the city. The man named Laverne Cavet had not even paid us a visit. I hoped he and Walter would stay away, for I had all I could do now with the work Celina had provided.

My hand grew tired from all the writing I had to do. Everything had to be answered, even the most trivial of notes. I had no idea of what was in store for me, but I did know for certain that, whatever return this work would provide, I would earn it.

On the fourth morning Walter stormed into the kitchen while I was eating. He wore riding breeches and a pale yellow shirt. He was booted, carried a crop and flailed at his boots with it exactly the way his father did.

"You're not very early," he said. "Put on riding clothes. Marie had some. I'll expect you to meet me downstairs in twenty minutes."

"To go riding?" I exclaimed.

"What else, woman? Riding, of course."

"But I have to see what your mother wishes of me. . . ."

"She wishes for you to ride with me. Get on with it. I hate riding when the sun gets too hot."

Again, I was deprived of a full breakfast, but I hurried

42

upstairs to find the riding habit and get into it. I thought Marie had excellent taste in clothing, if not in men, for this was a fetching outfit. It consisted of rather heavy tweed in a hip-fitting, long jacket, double breasted, with wide lapels. Beneath this I wore a white shirtwaist with a starched, close-fitting collar. The shirt was voluminous, but quite plain. All of this was crowned with a shiny top hat that I had to pin tightly to my hair.

The boots were as shiny as Walter's and there was a quirt, also provided with the outfit. When I descended the stairs, Walter waited at the landing, looking terribly impatient, but his face lighted up when he saw me, which I took as a compliment. I wasn't wrong.

"By heaven," he said, "you're a remarkably fetching woman, Jana. Marie's riding outfit looks extremely well on you. Better than it did on her."

"Thank you," I said.

"I hope you are a good rider, because I like something more than a mere canter across the pastures. If you can't keep up with me, I won't ask you again."

I had few doubts about my ability as a rider, but I merely inclined my head in acknowledgment of his warning. We walked to the stables along a cobbled path curving artistically between formal flower gardens. Men working about the estate didn't look up as we passed by. I would have complimented them on the excellence of the flowers, but refrained because I doubted it would meet with Walter's approval.

The horses were ready: a sleek, likely-looking mare for me and a russet brown stallion for Walter. We mounted, I a bit clumsily, for it had been some time since I'd ridden. Walter sliced at the stallion's flank with his quirt and he went charging at full speed across the level ground. I used my heels to get my horse into motion, and I did not insist upon all that speed. Walter had to pull up and wait for me.

"You're too slow," he said. "Are you afraid?"

"I see no point in exhausting my horse," I said.

43

"Oh, you don't!"

As he spoke he brought his quirt down on the flank of my horse as hard as he could lash out with it. The mare was off like a shot, with Walter riding right behind. When he got close enough he'd use his quirt on my horse as well as his own and he was laughing at my antics in trying to keep from being pitched out of the saddle.

I thought Walter was in sore need of a lesson. Out of the corner of my eye I saw him raise the quirt for another slash at my horse. Before he could bring it down, I sent my horse sharply to my right, cutting directly in front of him and causing his stallion to rear up in sudden fright. I now used my own quirt, but lightly, to try and make the mare understand what I expected of her. She seemed to cooperate well, for we streaked off, far ahead of Walter.

He shouted and came after me, but my smaller animal was the faster and we left Walter well behind until I saw a stone fence, a perfect jump. I sent the mare straight at it. The animal made a graceful leap over the barrier, soon followed by Walter whose horse was clumsier.

I turned mine sharply and headed back. The heavier stallion would be well winded by now, while my mare was still going strong. As I passed Walter, who was hanging on as I had at the outset, I called to him to follow me if he dared. My horse cleared the jump nicely, even from this short distance to prepare for the leap. I pulled up to watch Walter's stallion clear it, but clumsily, and when the horse came down after the jump, it was with such a hard impact that Walter was tossed from the saddle. He landed well. This was probably not the first time he'd been thrown.

I guided my horse to the stallion. I led the animal over to where Walter was dusting himself off and glaring somewhat balefully at me.

"You do not ride well, Mr. Ducan," I said. "That was an easy jump."

Before he could reply, I was heading back to the stables.

44

He didn't catch up with me until I'd dismounted and turned the horse over to a groom.

He dismounted and walked up to me. "That," he said "was not funny. If you dare laugh. . . ."

"I wouldn't think of it, Mr. Duncan," I said. "You had an unfortunate accident, that's all. Thank you for an interesting ride. I must now see to the needs of your mother. Good morning, sir."

He didn't walk me back to the house. I didn't take time to change, but proceeded directly to Mrs. Duncan's suite. She was still in bed; she rarely arose before eleven, and she had more notes and letters for me to handle, besides a long list of other duties, mostly trivial. I suspected she spent considerable time thinking them up.

If she noticed my riding costume, she didn't comment on it. She merely gave me my letter writing assignment and the list of other items.

"Your son and I enjoyed a brisk ride this morning," I said.

"I suppose you did." She looked at me searchingly. "Did he unseat you?"

"Why no," I said. "In fact, he was thrown himself."

"Much to your amusement, no doubt?"

I allowed myself a broad smile. "I did laugh, I'm afraid. He was not injured, of course."

"You may go," she said.

I thought she was angry that Walter had not sent me flying from my horse. It had been his obvious intention to do so if the mare could have been goaded into it—and I'd given him the opportunity to stay close enough so he could accomplish this amusement he apparently doted on. I felt that, for once, Walter had been put in his place. Whatever came of it, I wouldn't be sorry.

I worked diligently the rest of the day. At late afternoon Augusta Flores entered the library where I did most of my letter writing. She sat down and picked up one of the letters I'd written.

"A fine hand, my dear. Really the best I have ever seen. Your education was certainly not neglected."

"Thank you," I said. A compliment in this household was rare enough to be savored.

"I have a message for you from my sister. Tonight you will dine with us. Be sure to dress for the occasion. I think a pale green would look well and I recall that Marie favored that color, so there must be a selection for you to choose from."

"Whatever brought this on?" I asked, feeling I could be free with Augusta, for she had displayed nothing but kindness and friendship so far.

"Laverne will arrive soon."

"Laverne Cavet," I said. "I haven't met him yet. I'm quite honored."

"There are changes being made, my dear. These are at Claude's order and will not be countermanded by anyone. I'm not sure my sister agrees, but she is compelled to follow along. You may postpone the rest of your work to come upstairs with me. I've something to show you."

I followed her upstairs where she led me to one of the unused suites. When she opened the door, I discovered that all of my things had been moved here. I was now to enjoy two spacious rooms, beautifully furnished, and a full view of the front of the estate. It was a suite that must have been assigned to important guests.

"You will live here from now on," she said with a smile at my astonishment. "It seems, my dear, you have been accepted as a member of the family instead of the household. What brought this about, I have no idea. Or if I did have, I wouldn't tell you. I hope you will be happy here, Jana. I, for one, am delighted."

"Thank you," I said. "I'm quite overwhelmed."

"Don't let me delay you," she warned. "Supper will be at seven and you don't have too much time. I'm off to get ready myself."

I closed the door and examined my suite. The parlor was done in pale blue. The carpet was thick and luxurious.

46

There were two easy chairs, a small sofa in brocaded cover of blue and yellow.

In the bedroom I found a four poster, canopied in white, a long bureau, a vanity table, chairs and a very nice bathroom provided with a large mirror that was as clear as the one in my old room had been wavy.

I didn't take time to wonder why this had come about. Perhaps I'd misjudged this family and they'd been merely trying me out, to see if I had the poise and the proper character to join the family. I hadn't a single illusion that this was going to cut down on the work expected of me, for I knew by now that no member of this family gave anything away without expecting to be rewarded several times over in one way or another.

I brushed out my hair first and then assembled my evening dress. The petticoat was heavily laced and over it I wore the pale green gown which was far more elaborate than I'd expected, for it was of fine satin embroidered in a floral pattern. It was cut on the cross, the new method in dressmaking, so that it fitted snugly and was especially smooth around the hips.

I surveyed myself in the long mirror and I was satisfied that I would not disgrace this, or any, supper table. I added a touch of color to my cheeks and lips, toned it down with rice powder, tucked in a few stray strands of hair and, at exactly five minutes of seven, I was ready.

I was also the last to appear, for they were all in the reception hall waiting for me. I took my time descending the stairs, wishing to make as good an impression as possible. I saw Augusta, in the background, smile and nod heavily, an indication that I looked very well indeed. Only one of the others made a gesture of approval. As Walter moved to the foot of the stairs to receive me and escort me to the dining room he was rudely pushed to one side by a man I'd not seen before, but whom I assumed to be La-verne Cavet. He was tall, slim, his hair almost gray, though there was a great deal of it. He wore a Vandyke in a becoming manner and his attitude toward me was

47

one of graciousness as he presented his arm and tucked my hand under it.

"Remarkable," he said softly.

"May I inquire what seems to be remarkable?" I asked.

Claude bustled closer and interrupted any answer. "My dear Jana, this is my lifelong friend and confidant, Laverne Cavet, who is honoring us with his presence this evening."

"I'm pleased to meet you." I inclined my head toward my escort.

"What I was about to say," Laverne spoke loudly enough so all could hear, "is that I regard it remarkable that one related to this family, even as distantly as you, could be so attractive."

This was a compliment I didn't know how to answer, without seeming to agree in the insult to the Duncans' looks.

"It's not really to be wondered at, however," he went on. "I knew your mother and you look much as she did when she turned me down for the man who became your father. You may assume my disappointment was in such proportion that I have never married, preferring to remain alone that I might keep the memory of your mother intact."

"What a nice thing to say." I smiled.

"Now that the compliments have been dispensed with," Celina said, "I suggest we go at once to the table."

Apparently she didn't approve of Laverne's compliments. Laverne led me to the dining room and seated me; Odette entered ahead of the maids who would serve. She gave me a flashing glimpse of a look of dark anger, but that was all. Claude's edict that I be accepted as a member of the family didn't seem to have met with unanimous approval.

Augusta began the conversation so it would include me from the start. "Do you like your new suite, Jana?"

"It's lovely," I said. I looked from Celina to Claude. "I thank you with all my heart."

"I'm glad you're pleased," Celina said without warmth.

Claude, on the other hand, was quite expansive. "After all, your father was my cousin and we have discovered for ourselves that you are worthy to be part of this family. I wish to announce that I have reserved our stall at the opera for tomorrow evening. We shall dine at the hotel first. Please be prepared to leave here at three o'clock." He looked around the table. "Is that understood?"

We all said we would be ready. Then he sprang another surprise, one which I doubted even Claude's wife was prepared for.

"And we will soon give a formal dinner and ball here at Duncan House. In honor of our charming Jana."

I was so surprised I sat there stunned into silence, while Celina also recovered from the shock brought on by that statement. I finally found my voice.

"Mr. Duncan, I have been here such a short time, there is little need for all this trouble."

"It's not trouble, my girl. We like formal dinners and dances. Have them often. The best way for you to meet our friends. The ball will be held next Saturday."

"Then I'm grateful," I said with just the proper amount of humility.

"A great idea," Laverne approved.

"I think it's wonderful," Augusta said.

"Be sure you obtain the proper music," Walter advised. "The last chamber trio was out of a century ago."

Celina had the final word on the affair. "It's very well for all of you to make suggestions, but the preparations are upon my shoulders. I will have to work quickly. The time is so short."

"Mrs. Duncan," I said, "may I help? I've had good training in such matters."

"I fully expect you to help," she said crossly. "Whatever gave you the idea I could do it alone? Augusta is of no help."

"I might be, if you didn't criticize everything I did," Augusta said sharply.

Claude put an end to the argument. "It's settled then. Be sure to make this a sumptuous affair."

At the end of the meal, as usual, Claude, Laverne and Walter retired to the drawing room for brandy and cigars. The ladies remained at the table, though there was singularly little conversation between us. Celina still seemed angry at being informed of the dance with so little warning, and Augusta still smarted under her sister's unnecessary barbs. I did my best to carry on a conversation by talking about possible decorations for the affair.

I had been thoroughly trained in this at the finishing school where they taught everything well that concerned wealth and gracious living, and nothing about how one might make that living. So my ideas were good enough us were in deep discussion.
to capture Celina's attention and before long, all three of

When I retired for the night, I was still amazed at the sudden change of my status in this household. An elaborate ball and dinner in my honor? Celina was going to invite fifty couples, near capacity for this house. Tomorrow I would write the invitations and they would be delivered by hand before sunset.

At least tonight my sorrow, which returned every evening as I made ready for bed, was softened by my anticipation of the affair. It was going to be a busy week. The invitations to write and keep track of. A gown to select and be sure it was suitable. The opera which called for formal dress tomorrow evening. Dinner in the city. There'd scarcely be time for me to think.

However, as usual, just before I closed my eyes I thought about David. I would have done anything to get him included in this affair, but of course his name couldn't possibly be on the list. He was as much a stranger in New Orleans as I had been. I wanted to see him again, because he'd done so much for me. And I liked him. He was witty and charming, a man with a great deal of poise. I also guessed he might be worrying about me, being in no position to discover what had really happened to me.

I did wish to see him again, equally as much as I looked forward to the opera and the ball. Perhaps. I thought pleasantly, there might be more of a reason why I wanted to be with him again.

Perhaps I was falling in love with him. On this foolish note I curled up and prepared to sleep.

Five

Celina insisted the laundaulette be used in the journey to the city. As it would seat only four comfortably, with the evening gowns as lavish and bulky as those Celina and Augusta wore, Walter suggested he would drive me in the carriage. I had no objection, though I wondered why he suddenly became so willing to help.

It was a memorable occasion for me. Even the ball in my honor would hold no more importance, for I'd learned from Augusta just how vital it was to be seen at the opera. She'd warned me to select the best gown in Marie's wardrobe.

I still felt as if I were a charity case, using these garments bought for someone else, but I decided to be sensible about it, for everything was fresh and new. Marie, evidently, hadn't used them much. From their style, she couldn't have been missing too long, for these gowns were still the rage and had not gone out.

There were two types, one with a large wire frame bustle that was supposed to be cooler and healthier to wear than the old-style horsehair types. The other was the aesthetic style gown, altogether different and so new that they'd not yet been universally adopted, as had the new type of bustle. I decided to wear the aesthetic type at the ball and the bustle to the opera.

The gown itself was entirely of lace and must have taken months to make. It was of soft pink, trimmed with brown, and the contrast was quite pleasant to the eye. It was low cut, baring the shoulders.

I suspended work before noon and took a great deal of time with my toilette so that when it was time to go,

I was thoroughly satisfied that I would present as good an appearance as anyone at the opera.

Again it was Laverne who complimented me lavishly. Augusta was less enthusiastic in deference to her sister. It was apparent to me that Augusta was afraid of the Duncans. I didn't blame her. There were times when I felt uneasy with them.

"If we are quite ready," Claude said, impatiently as usual.

Walter led me to the carriage. The hostler had thoughtfully fastened the isinglass curtains in place to save my gown from the red dust from the dirt road all the way into the city. For added protection I draped a mantle around my shoulders, though the afternoon was blazing hot.

As he was expected to, Walter waited until the laundaulette began the journey. A coachman in a scarlet uniform held the reins and the small procession of two vehicles assumed a stately appearance because we were all so stylishly and expensively dressed.

A mile away from the mansion and the plantation, the road widened where there was a spring at which horses were allowed to drink. Without any warning to me, Walter pulled the carriage over, passed the laundaulette and kept going at a fast clip. I said nothing. Walter's actions were usually unpredictable and there was little sense in questioning them.

I had no idea what he was up to until he removed the whip from its socket and lashed out at the horses. They went into a fast run that became a gallop during which the carriage swerved wildly and sometimes threatened to tip over. None of this dismayed Walter who kept applying the whip.

I hung onto whatever I could grip well. I was being tossed about so that I was unable to protest. I doubted it would have done any good if I had. Walter was roaring with laughter and when he saw my frantic efforts to keep from being pitched out, curtains and all, his laughter became more boisterous.

This went on for more than two miles until we neared the city and other vehicles were on the road. Walter was then forced to slow down, but he did pass one farm wagon in a careless manner that almost got our left wheel locked in soft dirt off the road. The farmer, startled out of his wits, shook his fist at us.

Finally the sweating horses were allowed to proceed at a normal speed. I brushed dust off my gown, shook more of the mantle, and wondered if there was anything left to my hairdo. If I'd disliked Walter before, I hated him now.

"May I ask what was the meaning of that?" I asked.

"I thought you liked to ride fast. You didn't mind when you galloped across the fields and made me get thrown."

"So that's it," I said. "This is your revenge. You might have chosen another time. It's important to me, and to your father, that I look my best. You have nearly ruined my gown. If I'm asked about it, I shall tell your father what happened."

"He'd think it was funny," Walter said lightly.

"Your mother might not be of the same opinion."

"Mama thinks everything I do is funny. Go ahead and tell them."

I had no idea Walter was this childish. There was scant reason to argue with him. If I let my temper get away from me, my whole evening might be spoiled and I had a special reason why it should not be.

Laverne had brought along a New Orleans newspaper which I'd read thoroughly and found what I looked for. David Brennan was to be the guest conductor at tonight's opera. This news made me look forward to the evening with even more anticipation. David had rarely been out of my thoughts.

"I would ask you to be more careful during the rest of the journey, Mr. Duncan, for if you are not, I will never ride with you again. Have some consideration for the team, if not for me."

55

"I didn't like you at first," he said candidly, "but I'm beginning to now."

"I'm not complimented," I said. "How can you expect me to admire a man who does the silly things you do, to either embarrass or frighten me?"

"Marie used to say the same thing," he confided. "Once, when I drove like mad, she hit me on the head with her parasol. I made sure you weren't carrying one."

We were within the city limits now and the streets were busy with people and various kinds of vehicles, all apparently vying with one another for the same part of the road and the sidewalk.

"Why did Marie leave you?" I asked.

He said, "She didn't . . . . I wouldn't let any woman . . ." Then he stopped short. "I guess she didn't like me any more."

I had no comment so I remained silent and Walter promptly sulked.

At least he was good enough to wait in front of the restaurant until the laundaulette arrived. Then he helped me down to join the others while he followed the other vehicle to a nearby stable.

"Walter lost no time in getting here," Claude commented.

"No sir," I said. "He drove extremely fast."

"Scared you some, eh?" Claude asked with a smile. "Walter likes to scare people. I don't know why, but he dotes on it."

"Walter is young and full of spirit," Celina said in defense of her son. "You cannot expect him to be staid at his age."

In my opinion Walter was long out of his boyhood days, and should have known better, but I held my tongue.

We were to dine at the St. Charles. I, of course, had never heard of this fashionable hotel, nor of the fame its dining room had developed, but I soon discovered how great it was.

When our party walked through the lobby, every attendant swarmed in our direction. We were bowed to by a score of people, others looked envious, some showed traces of hatred in their eyes, but the sum total of all this only served to express the importance with which Claude Duncan was held.

A large center table, decorated with flowers, had been reserved for us. Six waiters and two captains stood by, for our benefit alone.

"Mademoiselle is lovely tonight," one of the captains whispered as he seated me.

We were not given menus. Claude had arranged everything beforehand. We were first served drinks. The women were served gin fizz, made with flower water and deceptively easy to drink. The men were given tall glasses of Planters Punch, an aromatic rum drink.

The first course was a light soup followed by filet of trout and then plump chicken cooked in claret. At first dinner was constantly interrupted by men who came to our table to greet Claude, until his exasperation caused him to issue an edict that no one else be allowed to approach the table. The captains enforced it, whispering to those who came to pay what I could only regard as homage.

Through it all Walter appeared bored and restless. Claude and Laverne were engaged in business talk and I joined Augusta and Celina in a lively discussion of fashions.

At eight I grew concerned that we'd be late for the opera, but I had no cause to worry, because I discovered later they actually held up the curtain until Claude Duncan and his party were seated in their center stall.

The French Opera House was at St. Louis and Bourbon Streets, an imposing, gray-walled building before which lines formed early in the afternoon for the evening performance.

"Often," Augusta informed me, "the performances outside the theatre are better than that inside. Small boys dance for coins, groups sing, others play instruments, all for the entertainment of the audience seeking seats in the *troisièmes* or the *quatrièmes*."

"The third level, and the chicken coop, the fourth," Laverne added gaily. "Opera is a serious business here. Quite the most important and best attended amusement the city enjoys."

"We have had famous operas performed here for the first time," Augusta boasted.

"And some sour ones," Claude added.

"We are being observed," Celina remarked from behind the folds of her fan. "Claude, be good enough to bow to the messieurs. They are actually waving."

Claude stood up and bowed elaborately. I wasn't paying much attention. The musicians had taken their places, ushers were going about extinguishing the gas lights. At any moment the conductor would appear. "David Brennan, Conductor," the posters outside the theatre had read. I felt great pride in the fact that I knew him.

The audience recognized the signal of the extinguished lights and the restlessness, the bowing and waving came to a halt. There was a flutter of applause as David came into the pit. He turned and bowed. He looked so handsome in his evening dress—and I'd thought of him as not being very handsome. He faced the stage, raised his baton and began the overture to the opera *Mignon*, which Augusta informed me, had enjoyed its première performance right here in this theatre fourteen years ago. A memorable night, I was told, and I didn't doubt it, but this one was far more memorable to me.

David conducted with an easy grace, without the often used flamboyant gestures and wavings of the arms which had no meaning except to impress the audience. If he was nervous, he showed no trace of it.

The overture was quite long and all through it the audience was silent and attentive. When it was over and David turned to bow, he received an ovation I was proud of.

"He is good," Claude commented.

"He's splendid," Laverne said. "This young man is going far. We should make sure, by lucrative contracts, that he goes no farther than New Orleans. We need him here after last season, when the director was so miserable."

"Did you like the conductor?" I asked Celina. Her word would go further than her husband's in the realms of New Orleans society.

"Yes, I must confess he surprised me, because he is such a young man. I don't believe I ever heard the Mignon overture played so well."

"That makes me very happy," I said, in a voice I knew must sound dreamy.

"Oh?" Celina arched an eyebrow at me. "What makes you say that?"

"I know him. He is the man who rescued me from the packet just before it sank. He brought me ashore and remained with me until we reached the city. He was very kind."

"We'll go backstage after the performance and you may introduce us to the gentleman," Laverne said expansively. "I agree, he is outstanding. New York will be bidding for him soon, you can bank on that."

"We'll keep him here," Claude said firmly. "I shall see to it."

"He must be more than just a good conductor," Walter observed. "The way Jana closed her eyes and sighed as he conducted . . . *M'sieur* Brennan must have a way with women."

He was taunting me, but I didn't mind. I was even interested to know I had closed my eyes and sighed, because I'd not been aware of it. The curtain was raised, the music swelled and the performance began. I soon became lost in its beauty, but never so deeply that I didn't watch David as much as I did the soprano and the tenor.

At the end of the act, the gas lights were again burning and the audience arose to stretch and to stroll through the halls, the Green Room, the bar. On every side I

59

heard comments about David's skill and I was never so pleased in my life.

We were, obviously, the most important group in the theatre. I half expected some of the women who approached us to curtsy. I was presented to many people, though not to all, and I sensed that I met only the more important ones. I overheard comments about my gown too. I'd been worried that Marie might have worn it here, but apparently if she had, no one recognized it.

The second act was rewarded with a standing ovation, many bouquets of flowers, the stamping of feet and shrill whistling. The New Orleans audiences were not bashful in showing approval. I was so happy for David, because I knew he must have been worried about his reception and now it was absolutely assured.

After the performance I grew impatient while Claude shook hands with so many people and Celina engaged in brief conversations with an array of diamond-laden matrons. Walter ignored the whole thing and took no pains to show he was bored. Laverne was as active in greeting friends as Claude, but Augusta seemed to find it difficult to be as effusive as her sister and remained, for the most part, in the background. When she did come forward to greet an old friend, however, she did so with genuine enthusiasm.

Laverne said, "We'd best go meet this young conductor whom Jana knows. Before he leaves the theatre."

"I sent word he was to remain," Claude said. "There is no need to hurry."

If he only knew how I felt, he'd have sped through the crowds shouting for them to clear the way. As it happened we spent another fifteen minutes in the lobby. No one was in any hurry to end the evening.

Finally Laverne led us to the stage entrance. A doorman bowed civilly and let us through the group waiting to claim the attention of the stars. I was not interested in them.

I saw David at the same moment he spotted me. He raised both arms and waved lustily as he threaded his way through the crowd. It was strange. Even months afterwards I realized that at the moment we approached one another, no one else was in the theatre. Without the slightest hesitation he enfolded me in his arms and to my great delight, didn't let me go for a long time. Had there been fewer people, I'm sure he would have kissed me.

"You're so beautiful," he whispered.

"They're saying great things about your ability," I returned the compliment. "Oh, David, it's so wonderful to see you again."

"My dear Jana," Claude touched my shoulder, "it's time you introduced us to this young man."

I introduced him all around. For some reason I thought Claude had grown cold in his enthusiasm for David's conducting. And Celina was haughtier than ever. Walter remained bored, but I thought I detected a look of anger in his eyes. Laverne and Augusta were properly appreciative and said so.

"I understand we owe Jana's life to your courage," Augusta said.

David shook his head slowly. "It was an awful few moments. I did little. There was nothing anyone could do."

"You have our gratitude," Claude said stiffly. I wondered what was the matter with him.

David had never shown any shyness and he now took both my hands in his. "I tried to find you," he said. "No one had seen you."

"The probate judge did," said Walter harshly. "She was going to be put in jail as an indigent until she thought of asking my father for help."

David's smile faded momentarily and there was plain anger in his eyes as he looked at Walter. Then he relaxed.

"Everything turned out all right," he said. "I'm glad. Jana suffered enough. I shall look forward to seeing all of you again—and often," he addressed me. "I have to go now. There is some sort of reception for the cast and I'm to be there, though I'd rather be with you, Jana. Good night. Thank you for coming to see me."

Then he was gone, but I was in an ecstasy that would last for days. I was in love with him and I knew it beyond the slightest doubt. I felt that he loved me too. I felt it in his embrace and in every word he spoke, every look he cast my way.

Someone took my arm. I wasn't sure who. I floated out of the theatre. We enjoyed a late supper at Antoine's and his glorious food might as well have been sawdust for all the attention I gave it. During the long ride back, this time in the landaulette, for Laverne rode with Walter, I had little to say. Claude seemed quieter than usual too, but Augusta kept up a ceaseless chatter with her sister, mostly about the opera and people they'd seen there.

It was not too far from dawn when we arrived home, but for all of me it could have been daylight. This had been the happiest evening of my life. I even kissed Claude in appreciation, which rather startled him.

My world had suddenly grown bright again.

Six

So began the change in my social position at Duncan House. I was now an approved member of the clan. I had my new suite, I dined with the family, I was even given a substantial sum of money with which to gratify my own needs for new clothes and whatever necessities were required.

There was only a short time to the weekend when the ball was to be held, but my fears that there wouldn't be sufficient time were removed somewhat. There'd been so many of these social events at Duncan House that the preparations were more or less routine. Still, there was much to do and my part was to see to the invitations, which had been dispatched, and to arrange for food and drink.

The day before the affair Claude didn't go into the fields, nor to the office he maintained in New Orleans. Instead he stayed home to be of help, though no one seemed to find anything for him to do. Late in the morning he sent for me. Coleen found me in one of the guest rooms helping to prepare it.

"The master, mum, he sent me looking for you. You're to come at once to the library."

"What in the world does he want now?" I asked, dismayed at the interruption.

"I don't know, mum, but he's in a fine mood so I wouldn't worry any that something's gone wrong."

"I can be glad of that," I commented. "I'll be right down."

I did take the time to remove the large apron which covered my dress, and to wash dust off my hands and face before I hurried to the library. Claude was behind his desk, chair tilted back, looking very much at ease.

"Sit down, my dear," he invited. There was none of the usual brusqueness about him this morning. "It's time we had a talk."

I wondered about what, but I obeyed him and seated myself. He rolled his usual thin cheroot between his fingers before taking a long, thoughtful puff on it. He let the smoke out slowly while his eyes studied my face with an almost embarrassing intentness.

"Are you quite happy here?" he began.

"Yes, sir. I can say that without any qualification."

"I'm pleased, Jana. You know I admired your father, and your mother as well. I feel that it is my duty to take their place with you, if I can. Therefore, I wish you to come to me with any problems, or for any advice you may seek."

"Thank you, Mr. Duncan," I said, wondering what had brought this on. It wasn't fair to compromise his apparent kindness with such thoughts, but Claude was the kind of a man who always had a motive and it was not usually one to benefit the person he dealt with.

"Did you enjoy the opera?"

"Oh yes, very much."

"The young conductor seemed attracted to you. Or was I wrong about that?"

"I hope he was," I said frankly. "I owe him a great deal. My very life, to be explicit."

"Is that the only reason you like him?"

"I believe him to be a kind and gentle person with the ability to go far in his field."

"If he succeeds in New Orleans, he will be accepted anywhere."

"Then I pray he succeeds beyond his own hopes."

"That is up to him. Now I understand that you went riding with Walter a few days ago and the experience was not one you enjoyed. Am I correct?"

"I'm afraid you are."

"I know what happened. I recall the way he drove the carriage to the city the afternoon of the opera. Walter likes to frighten people and to play tricks. It is a failing I have been unable to change in him, but he is not deliberately vicious."

"I sincerely hope not," I said. I couldn't bring myself to lie and agree with him entirely.

"He feels badly that you will not ride with him again."

"But, Mr. Duncan, I have not said that. I don't even know that he has gone riding since."

"He has, every day. He's taking the stallion out this afternoon. He does not like riding alone. I haven't the time, but if you would be so kind. . . ."

I couldn't deny him that favor. Walter was a selfish boor, a man I cared little for, but he was no demon. Then too, he was an important member of the family which, apparently, I'd just joined.

"I'll be glad to ride with him," I said.

"That's fine," Claude smiled expansively. "I know that boy will make me proud of him yet. He has the ability. After all, he is my son."

"I'm sure you'll be proud of him," I said.

"Of course I will. One day he'll inherit everything I have, which is considerable, as you likely know. You will ride with him then?"

"I shall get ready at once."

"Good. Don't tell him I asked you to do this. Sometimes he's quite sensitive about such matters."

I agreed. Claude brought his chair forward and began inspecting some of the papers on his desk—a signal that I was dismissed. I left him and went upstairs to tell Augusta that I would not be available to help for part of the afternoon.

"I'm going riding with Walter," I explained.

"Indeed?" She looked surprised. "I thought the last time was enough."

"I don't think he'll repeat that silliness. Anyway, the air will do me good."

"You just came from talking to Claude, didn't you?"

"Why, yes."

"I understand, dear. Run along. We'll get by without you. A fat lot of good it would do us if we didn't."

I knew what she meant, but I didn't comment. I went to my rooms and changed into my riding habit. Dinner would not be served for another two hours, so there was sufficient time for a good ride. Odette informed me that Walter had already gone to the stables, so I made my way there in time to reach him before he had ridden off.

"Please understand me, Walter," I said. "I like riding and, like you, enjoy it more when someone is along. But if you repeat any of the antics you displayed last time, I will never again ride with you."

He scowled and when he did this he looked amazingly like his father. "Come along or not, as you please, but don't threaten me, do you hear? I won't stand for it."

Had it not been for his father, and my position in this household, I would have walked away from him. However, I didn't comment, but I went into the stable and asked a hostler to saddle the same mare I'd used before.

By the time she was ready and I led her outside, I found that Laverne had joined us, but not to ride apparently, because he wasn't dressed for it.

"Good afternoon, Jana," he said. "You're very lovely today."

"Thank you, sir," I gave him a proper smile. "Coming, Walter?"

"You go along," Walter said, "I've some business to talk over with Laverne. Won't take but five minutes or so."

"I'll see you at the jump," I told Walter. I set out across the fields at a sedate pace. I was occupied with trying to make up my mind as to exactly what Claude was up to. My horse broke into a canter and I then occupied myself with my riding. I looked back, but Walter wasn't in sight yet. I'd crossed one large field and I was approaching the stone wall where I'd jumped before. I headed the mare directly toward the same spot and urged her to a faster pace.

She was an intelligent animal and seemed to know what I wanted, and to enjoy it as much as I. She raced toward the wall, lifted easily and gracefully, and cleared the wall just before she gave a violent sideways twist of her body.

I felt myself slipping out of the saddle so I threw myself clear before the mare went down on her side, sliding with maddening pain along the rough ground.

I had the breath knocked out of me so that I was unable to get up immediately, though I tried to. At first I thought the mare had injured herself, but she finally struggled to her feet and stood quivering while I finally managed to get up.

I stroked her neck and head, spoke quietly to her, though I felt little of this assurance myself. I was looking at a large tree branch, long dead and dried, which had been pulled directly behind the stone wall. It was large enough to make the jump impossible and provided with enough jagged branches to make it downright dangerous. The mare had seen all this as she cleared the wall and instinctively threw herself to one side, which probably saved her from a broken leg or neck, and me from injuries which could have been just as severe.

So this, I thought, was why Walter had wanted me to ride with him. He'd even gone to his father to have him urge me to go riding again so this could happen. Had the mare been hurt, my anger would have been boundless. It wasn't Walter's fault that she was not, nor that I hadn't broken my own neck.

When Walter did appear, he was riding casually and he made no attempt to put his horse into a run to leap the wall. Instead he cantered up to it. I will admit that when he saw the large branch hidden behind the wall, he seemed startled.

"Who put that there?" he demanded. "What are you trying to do, get me killed?"

I curbed my anger once again. "I did not place that branch there, Walter. I do not know who did, but it was deliberate."

"Now don't you go blaming me," he said angrily. "You probably set it as a trap for me."

"Would I be apt to take the jump if I placed that branch there? Can't you see where the mare's hoofs plowed up the grass and where I landed when she threw me?"

Walter rose in the saddle to peer about. He nodded glumly. "I guess you're right."

"Do you know who is responsible for that?" I demanded.

He nodded slowly. "Guess maybe I do. Lots of folks who live hereabouts come on Papa's property to hunt. Papa has ordered that nobody set foot on any land he owns, to either hunt or fish. Papa says hunters can get downright dangerous to field hands the way they shoot at anything that moves. Papa had half a dozen of them arrested a few weeks ago and the judge sent them to jail. I guess they got sore and decided to make trouble for us."

It sounded logical enough, but I was still suspicious of him. I had little faith in his honesty, but he could be right. I mounted and we began to ride. Not fast, and I wasn't going to make any jumps, no matter how attractive they seemed to be. The one thing I couldn't believe about Walter's story of poachers was that the branch had been placed exactly where I'd be expected to make my jump. Whoever placed it knew I'd selected this spot before and would likely do so again.

Walter was surprisingly subdued and he even tried to be pleasant. He talked horses, spoke of the races they often held in New Orleans, and even spoke of the opera, through which I could have sworn he dozed most of the time.

We were on our way back when Walter pulled up short

68

near a shady stand of tall oaks. "I want to talk," he said.

I dismounted obediently. We turned our horses free to graze and we entered the grove to enjoy the coolness of its shade. Walter sat down with his back against a tree trunk. He patted the ground beside him. I sat down and waited for him to begin. I could see that he had something on his mind.

"That orchestra conductor likes you, doesn't he?" Walter began.

"I hope so," I said.

"You like him too. I can tell."

"Of course I do. He saved my life."

"That wasn't gratitude I saw on your face when you met him. Not altogether."

"You're very observant," I said.

"If you're not in love with him you think you're going to be. Isn't that the truth?"

I studied his stern face for a moment. "Walter, that's none of your business."

"You're wrong. It is my business."

"Now, in what way would my feelings for a young man concern you?"

"You're going to marry me," he said simply.

I heard myself gasp in surprise. "Walter, whatever gave you that idea? I mean no offense, and probably I should be honored, but you must be fooling."

"I'm not fooling," he said sullenly. "I mean it. You're not going to marry this baton swinger. You're going to marry me."

"Walter, you are married. Have you actually forgotten that?"

"I haven't forgotten. Marie was no good. She couldn't bear children. It was expected of her and when she found out she couldn't, she ran away."

"That does not mean you are free to marry," I reminded him.

"Oh," he gestured carelessly, "Papa can fix that."

"Walter, you amaze me. You sit here and speak as if this was no more than a minor suggestion instead of something so impossible as to be fantastic."

"What makes you say that? There's nothing the matter with me. I'm going to be very rich and powerful some day."

"I'm not in love with you. I never could be. Isn't that important?"

"Marie wasn't in love with me either, but that didn't make any difference. Papa thought she was very sturdy, from a healthy stock, and she'd have fine children. He says you will too. He was wrong about Marie, but I think he's right about you."

"He is not," I said. "I may bear strong children. I hope to heaven I do, but not your children, Walter."

"You're in love with that musician."

"I do not intend to discuss that with you now. I want to go back, if I may."

"Go ahead. I'm going to stay here for awhile. Just don't get the idea into your head that you're not going to marry me, because you are.

He was beginning to intrigue me. He and his father. I settled back. "Walter, you know that Marie did not leave because she couldn't have children. What was the real reason?"

"I don't know. She just up and went. That's all."

"You haven't heard from her since?"

"No, not a word. She didn't even write her own folks."

"How long ago did she leave?"

"A year . . . no, not quite a year, but she's not coming back. I'm sure she won't. She'd be too scared of Papa."

"Was he responsible for her leaving?"

"I don't know. She never said, but Papa was awful mad when he found out she'd never give him a grandson."

"Has anyone ever tried to find her?"

"Papa said let her go. He was glad to be rid of her."

"I feel very sorry for the poor girl, but you are married to her until she is proven to be dead or sufficient time lapses so she can be declared dead."

"I said, Papa can fix that."

"What does your mother think of this absurd plan?"

"She wants me to get married again and have children, just as Papa does."

"What of your Aunt Augusta? How does she feel about it?"

"I don't know. She doesn't count anyway. She's just a poor relation living off Papa."

"Like me," I said.

"Yes, like you. Soon as he gets Marie properly dead, we'll talk about getting married. Of course, you'll have to bear up with my faults. Laverne says I got plenty. One of them could have been downright big trouble except for Laverne."

"Trouble over what?" I asked.

"Money. Gambling money. I like to gamble and everybody knows how rich Papa is, so they let me borrow all I want. But Papa said he wasn't going to square my debts any more and last week I lost a few thousand. Laverne just told me he was settling it up for me. He's a good friend."

I was suddenly tired of this conversation and I went after my horse. Walter remained where he was and by the time I was mounted and ready to ride back, I'll swear he was sound asleep. I thought him an impossible fool, but I did smile at the incongruity of the whole thing. This romantic affair certainly reached his heart. I was sure that he no more cared for me than I did for him. But who were we to defy the edicts of his father?

Now it was perfectly clear to me why I'd been promoted from the poor relation to a member of the family, given a suite of rooms, allowed to eat with the family, taken to the opera and now an elaborate ball was being prepared in my honor.

Claude wanted me to experience what his money would provide, so that I'd overlook the fact that his son was

71

an impossible creature and accept him as the price of the luxuries that would come my way.

I compared those benefits against real love. Anything that Claude Duncan offered me was a paltry thing compared to the warmth and the beauty of the kind of love I was sure David and I could share.

I understood now why Claude had been so prompted in taking me in when I was threatened with being jailed as an indigent. He must have recognized in me another chance for him to gain a grandchild.

All to provide Claude with the means to continue the Duncan dynasty. Had it not been so serious, so carefully planned, I'd have been inclined to laugh aloud at the absurdity of it.

I knew Claude's power, what his money and influence could do. I knew how ruthless the man was and how determined he could be to get whatever he wanted.

I didn't feel like laughing.

Seven

I had made up my mind not to say anything about Walter's unromantic approach to marriage. I tried to convince myself that the idea was his alone and he only insisted it was backed by his father to intimidate me into accepting. I soon realized this wouldn't work, however; I knew Claude Duncan was behind it all. After the dinner and ball, I would have to speak to him about this.

When I returned to the house that afternoon, I immediately plunged into the preparations which were behind the time to have everything finished.

All of us, save Walter and Claude, worked industriously to have things ready. On the day of the ball, more help arrived from New Orleans. We decorated the drawing room, now deprived of most of the furniture, with flowers. I decorated the little platform where the orchestra would play, with more flowers and bunting. How I wished David was invited. I didn't dare suggest he be, for he had little or no social standing with Celina or her friends.

I also made up my mind about something else. If Claude insisted I marry his son, I would have to leave this household. To do so, I must have work ready for me. I planned to visit New Orleans and try to find a job. After working for Celina Duncan as social secretary, I would be experienced enough to satisfy any of the many wealthy women who might be in need of this sort of help. Certainly I'd served Celina well, and she could find no fault with me. I felt that, having worked for her, I'd actually be in demand.

All that could come later. At the moment I had the

ball to occupy my time. Celina supervised, but carefully avoided anything that required physical effort. She was very good at directing the rest of us. Augusta worked diligently and well. Before the house was fully decorated, she and I had become good friends. I was tempted to tell her of Walter's ideas, but I decided it wouldn't be fair to burden her with something she could do nothing about. Walter made it quite clear they regarded Augusta as a poor relative living on the bounty Claude provided. She was in no more of a position to argue with the Duncans than I.

When I crept into bed that night, I was tired to the point of tears. A feeling augmented by the frustrations I faced, for upon sober reflection I came to wonder how I could defy Claude Duncan. The fact that I might be in love with someone else wouldn't matter to him. I was like one of his possessions. He could do with me whatever he liked.

Even if I'd never met David, to be married to a man like Walter was out of the question. I could never be in love with him. Like Marie, I would finally rebel and run away.

Calmness came when my thoughts turned to David and that wondrous moment when we saw one another backstage. Walter, his mother and his father, had no further meaning. No Duncan could make me give up my love for David. And my strength in making this decision came from the love I knew David felt for me.

In the morning I awakened early, which was good, because there proved to be many last-minute details to take care of. I talked with Odette and Silviana, the cook, about food and service. Everything was in order. Even Odette seemed anxious to make this a wonderful ball.

Laverne worked along with us, Augusta had a backache from standing on a foot ladder to tie bunting and attach Japanese lanterns to trees outside.

Walter never did put in an appearance, though I'd

expected that of him. Claude puttered around making a pretense of being helpful. Celina spent herself in giving orders, few of which were followed.

Finally we were done. Now it was time to prepare ourselves. Celina had vanished long before, presumably to begin dressing. I had skipped dinner. Most of us had, so I visited the kitchen and begged a cup of coffee. Laverne followed my example, but laced his with brandy. We seated ourselves in the dining room and relaxed.

"There are times," Laverne said, "when I wonder if it's worth it, and also what a bachelor like me is doing here anyway."

"You were of great help," I told him.

"I could name a couple of people who were not," he smiled. "Tell me, are you in love with that conductor?"

"Why do you ask?"

"Oh, it was the way you two seemed to discover one another in that busy backstage area. You saw him, he saw you, and neither of you saw anybody else. Am I correct?"

He was very observant, I thought. "We'd been through much danger together," I explained, "and we were uncommonly glad to see one another again."

"It was more than that. Naturally it's none of my business, except that I'm afraid . . . well . . . one does get into all sorts of difficulties trying to be a good fellow. I'd best shut up."

"Are you referring to the fact that Mr. Duncan wishes me to marry Walter so I can provide a grandson?"

He looked surprised. "You know about it? Don't tell me Claude has spoken! This was not the right time for it. He would wait until you were filled with admiration for his generosity and fully aware of what his money can do."

"Walter told me yesterday."

"When you went riding with him?" Laverne nodded knowingly. "That young man never could keep anything to himself."

75

"He was quite open about it," I said.

"He wouldn't know any other way. What are you going to do?"

"I may be trusting you too much, Mr. Cavet, but I am not going to marry Walter. I cannot think of anything worse than being married to him."

Laverne laughed softly. "He is a scoundrel. And they take full advantage of him in the city. I just cleared up an embarrassing gambling debt for him. If Claude knew of it, he'd have gone into a rage."

"What can I do? When I make my refusal known to Mr. Duncan, I'm sure I shall no longer be welcome here."

Laverne stroked his Vandyke and sipped his cooling coffee, redolent of brandy. "It's not a question of what you will do, my dear. You will find something. What should concern you more is that Claude may find a way to make you marry his son."

"No . . . no, Mr. Cavet. There is no such way. I can tell you that now."

"And I can assure you if there is a way, however remote, Claude will find it. Believe me, he is not a man to be trifled with. He is too rich and too powerful."

"Marie hasn't been missing very long, has she?" I asked.

"No . . . not a year yet."

"I guessed that because of the gowns she bought before she left. One of them is so stylish that it must have come from France and it is a fashion still not yet in vogue here. I'm going to wear it though. Poor Celina may be shocked, but it's a lovely dress."

"Then wear it," he said. "I'll look forward to seeing you in it."

"Thank you. I'd best begin to get ready. There will be so many last things to do."

"You go ahead. I'm staying right here until I feel more rested. I have to dress too, you know. At the moment I've never felt less like it. Run along."

I sent for hot water and bathed until the soreness

left my muscles. Then I began to dress. I'd already tried on the new aesthetic gown to be sure it fitted me well, which it did. I knew there were going to be lifted eyebrows and much comment when I appeared in it. I was about to break the silly style of bustles and lace petticoats, at least locally.

Before I put on the gown, I studied my hair arrangement and decided that must be different too, so I experimented with brushing some of it well forward down over my forehead, and I believed it looked well, so I left it that way.

I waited until the last minute to get into the gown, because it required but a few minutes. The fashions which would prevail at the ball required at least two hours to properly wear.

From my window I watched the carriages arrive. There was such a steady procession of them, I wondered how in the world all these people would get into the house, large as it was.

Coachmen drove around to the back where banquet tables had been set up for them and they'd be well provided with food and drink. I had made up my mind not to go down until the last possible moment. Not that I believed myself to be of such rare beauty that everything would come to a standstill when I appeared. I knew better than that, but I was going to astonish them. The women, at least, would stop their chattering for a few moments.

A closed carriage pulled up. The first man out was David. I gave a cry of happiness, for I'd never expected him. I didn't care what anyone else thought now. I slipped into the dress and gave myself a swift appraisal in the mirror.

It was a beautiful dress. More like a robe, of white silk embroidered with clusters of roses. The dress was loose and had very large sleeves. It fitted me sleekly and reminded me of engravings I'd seen of the style worn by medieval women. Had I not been slender I couldn't have worn it and I doubted it would ever become the rage in fashion, but for tonight it would be my gown and it would demand attention.

Marie evidently had shoes made to order for the dress, for they were of fabric, covered with the same rose-embroidered material, though the flowers were on a much smaller scale of course. The shoes were soft and without heels. I patted the hair over my forehead, decided I was now ready and I left my suite to walk slowly along the corridor to the stairway.

At the landing where the stairs curved, I stopped momentarily. I heard the female voices sputter and cease. As I finished descending the stairs, the reception hall became crowded when people jammed into it from the other rooms to find out what was causing the astonishment.

At the foot of the stairs Walter waited for me. The gown made no impression on him. Augusta was smiling broadly, but Celina's face was a mask of anger which she finally controlled and she began to smile as if nothing was wrong.

Laverne came forward, elbowing his way closer. "Absolutely astonishing," he whispered. "Everything! It's a beautiful gown on a no less beautiful girl. I can tell you that Claude said so too."

"Thank you," I said. "David is here. I'm sure I saw him."

"He is to lead the orchestra. A last-minute decision by Claude."

"Oh!" I knew I showed the disappointment I felt. "I'd hoped it was as a guest."

"Don't worry. He'll be circulating about. You'll have opportunities to be with him."

"Will you try to get Walter away?" I begged. "So I can go to David for a few minutes."

"I'll uncork a bottle of brandy and Walter will come running. Ah me, I wish I were younger. I'd throw David out of here bodily."

78

"You are nice," I said. "I'm afraid I've come to depend on you."

He patted my hand. "That's what I like to hear. A man wants to be appreciated, especially by a lovely girl. Go find your David."

That was not quite as simple as I believed. Celina trapped me near the drawing room door. With one of her sunny smiles, she presented me to many of her friends. All of them commented on the dress and not one had an adverse criticism.

"It's the latest," I explained. "From Paris, of course. I do believe we shall soon find dresses more comfortable to wear. I assure you this one is."

"At least you can sit down freely," one woman commented. "I've grown tired of being followed about by my bustle."

At last I was able to escape. I walked casually into the drawing room, nodding to people but never stopping and avoiding groups so that my progress to the orchestra stand was not impeded. David, in evening dress, was going over the music with the dozen musicians. He saw me, turned the pages of music over to one of the others and stepped down from the platform to meet me.

"It's so good of you to come, David," I said.

He laughed softly. "It wasn't exactly a matter of choice, Jana. I was practically ordered to lead the orchestra."

"I'm glad and beholden to whoever brought you here. Perhaps later we can manage to slip outside for a little while. The room will become very crowded and hot and I shall surely need to take the air. Watch me and when you leave, there is a path leading to a summer house a safe distance from the mansion. It's the only path that is paved with red brick, so you'll be sure to find me."

"I'll be there," he said. "Dear Jana, I never thought my luck would be this good. I'm to be contracted over a long period at a fat salary to remain in New Orleans and lead the French Opera. It's the chance of a lifetime, and

79

then . . . you came along to make my good fortune even greater. You'd best go now. Mr. Duncan is looking this way and not in approval from what I can see of his face."

As I turned away from David, Claude advanced toward me. To my vast relief, he called greetings to David and seemed quite friendly. He took my elbow and escorted me to a quiet part of the great room.

"We've found a great conductor in that young man. Every member of the orchestra tells us he is the best they ever worked under."

"How nice of you to say that, Mr. Duncan."

"He's a personable young man too. I can see that you are taken with him."

"Indeed, sir," I confessed, "I am. I like him."

"Isn't it possible you like him because he saved your life?"

"Oh yes, that too. But not that alone, sir." I thought it time to change the subject before something happened to spoil the evening. "Do you approve of my gown, Mr. Duncan?"

"It was the last thing Marie bought," he said. "I think she bought it to defy my wife and possibly anger her. I approve of it. You look very fashionable in it, but I daresay not many women would."

"I do hope she won't be offended," I said.

"She probably will be. It's almost time for dinner and I'd like you to meet a few more important people. Remember, this ball is in your honor. You and I will lead the grand march."

"I look forward to it," I said.

On our way to the dining room we stopped and I spoke to a number of people. Claude was temporarily drawn away by one of his friends. Celina noted this and quickly made her way to my side.

"I am dismayed by that awful gown," she whispered.

"Why, Mrs. Duncan, everyone thinks it quite lovely."

"I do not. Marie bought this in defiance of me. I should have cut it to pieces."

"But why?" I asked. "Is it not modest enough for you? My shoulders are not bared as yours are, nor is the cut at all low in comparison to yours. It does show my figure, I grant. . . ."

"Are you corseted, may I ask?"

"With this gown there's no need for it."

"You should be ashamed of yourself. I will not discuss this further."

"Would you like me to change?" I asked, without any intention of doing so.

"Certainly not. It would be too obvious. We'll go into dinner now. See that you behave like a proper lady. Even in that . . . that dress."

"Yes, Mrs. Duncan," I said dutifully.

Augusta was different, as I expected she v
"You've set tongues to wagging, young lady, affair is the better for it."

"Celina doesn't approve," I said.

"She hates that dress because it's different and because she could never wear it. Nor I," she added with a little sigh. "Mainly, however, she dislikes the dress because it must remind her of Marie. It was bought in defiance of Celina's wishes and she cannot stand that."

Several guests joined us to talk about the gown and they all admired it, so I didn't mind any longer what Celina's comments had been.

Then Walter elbowed his way toward me to give me his arm as we went in to dinner.

Eight

Claude and I led the grand march and enjoyed part of the first dance before I was claimed by another man. My dance card was full, but I would have to disappoint some of Claude's friends because I meant to see David alone, no matter what repercussions followed.

It was a wonderful evening for me and in a way I was grateful for it. I'd have appreciated it far more if I'd not known that Claude and Celina were setting the stage for my marriage to Walter by having me meet all their friends. To me it seemed they were promoting their own interests far more than mine.

Laverne claimed me for a dance just before the intermission was due. I had to trust him, for I did need help.

"Would you be kind enough to lead me to one of the French windows so that I might slip outside? I wish to meet David for a few moments when the intermission begins."

"You are in love with him," Laverne commented with a sad shake of his head. "It means trouble, Jana. I presume you are aware of that."

"I know, but I'm not afraid."

"The orchestra can start the dancing again without David being there. Who has the first and second dances after intermission?"

I studied my card. "Matthew Foley and Christopher Manning."

"I shall see to it they are so busy they will not make a fuss searching for you. Be back here for the third dance. I can't be responsible from then on."

"You are a dear," I said gratefully.

He steered me toward the far end of the room. I knew David was watching. Laverne opened the door for me and whisked me outside. I hurried along the path to the summer house, fortunately well isolated from the mansion and from the stables, where the coachmen were having their own food and drink.

A few moments after I reached the summer house I heard David hurrying toward me. He bounded up the four steps and I went into his arms as naturally as I had the time we met backstage. Neither of us spoke because at that moment words were unnecessary.

He let me go and stepped back, still holding my hands. "You are the loveliest woman in the world," he said.

"The luckiest," I countered his compliment. "Darling, I'm so happy that you've been accepted. I know how much that means to you."

"It has come to mean only one important thing. Now I can ask you to marry me."

"I will, David. I promise you."

He drew me to him. "Now everything in my life is complete. How soon will you marry me?"

I pressed my cheek against his and held him tightly. "There is no reason to wait long. I do appreciate what the Duncan's have done for me, but I cannot allow them to rule my life."

"Something tells me they are trying to," he said. "I heard a few whispers to the effect that some people feel sorry for you because you are destined to marry Walter. Is that true?"

"I would never marry Walter. I'm afraid, though, that he believes it, for he told me so quite frankly."

"I'm going to take you away from this house," David said. "You don't belong here."

"They've been kind to me. I must not forget that, even if their reasons were selfish. I don't want to create any trouble. Claude is too rich and powerful to be defied. I must make him understand that I'm in love with you."

"The old man wants grandchildren. That's it, isn't it?"

84

"Yes. He seems determined that the Duncan dynasty must be insured. Walter's first wife was unable to bear children."

"Has she ever been found?"

"No. Though I doubt anyone has taken the trouble to search for her. How much more time do we have?"

"A few minutes. Precious few."

"More than you think. Laverne is keeping the men on my card for the next two dances so busy, they won't even look for me."

"Good for him. What's his connection with this family?"

"So far as I know, he's an old friend. He's gone out of his way to help me."

"I can see that. You understand that Mr. Duncan is going to be very angry when he finds out you won't marry Walter. You have to be prepared for that."

"I am. My fears are mostly for you, darling. He has such a great amount of influence"

"I know, and he isn't reluctant to use it. He might even ruin my chances here. But there are other cities."

I sat down on the bench built against the wall of the summer house. "Why couldn't we have met under other circumstances?" I said. "Tragedy brought us together and misfortune seems to follow us. I'm afraid of Claude Duncan."

"Jana," his voice dropped to a whisper, "don't show any signs of alarm, but someone has been watching us for the last two or three minutes. I heard movement in the brush right behind you."

"If it's Claude. . . ." I said in horror.

"It wouldn't be Claude, but I want to find out who it is. I'm going after him."

"David, you may be hurt. . . ."

"I think I can take care of myself. Stand up now. I'm going to kiss you. Let's give the gentleman his money's worth before I teach him a lesson that it's improper to spy upon two people in love."

His kiss was long and ardent, but I was shaken and

beginning to tremble for fear that I had overstepped myself in meeting David this way. Claude was capable of high anger and roughshod methods against those he had cause to dislike. David could never stand up to this man and hope to come out of the battle without being badly hurt.

David suddenly let go of me, took a single long step across the summer house, vaulted the low rail, landed outside the open structure and raced toward the brush. I hurried down the steps, intent upon joining him.

I heard him cry out and there was the sound of an impact of bodies before the fight began. I heard angry voices. They were not David's, so there must be more than one man battling him. I called his name and rushed into the thin brush to search for him. I felt my gown snag on sharp branches, but I simply tore myself free. I moved about trying to find him. The struggle was over. David should have called to me, but all I heard was the crash of the brush as more than one person hurried away from the scene.

A low groan gave me directions and I soon found David trying to get up. It was too dark here to assess any injuries he might have, but there was no question that he'd been hurt.

"David . . . Dave, are you all right?" I asked. "Oh, darling, we must get you to a doctor. . . ."

He was on his feet by now. "I'm . . . all right. There were two of them and the second one must have used a club on my head. It feels as if it's falling off."

"We'll go back to the house. . . ."

"Wait! We can't do that. You go back. At once. In a few moments the orchestra will start the dancing again. I told them not to wait for me. I'll have a few minutes to clean up. Hurry! Go back. We can't let this get out of hand now."

I didn't agree with him. I no longer cared what anyone thought, but I respected his judgment and I did fear for him. I kissed him hurriedly and made my way back to

86

the house. I used the rear door, passed through the kitchen where the help was so busy nobody took time to notice my disheveled appearance. I reached my suite and took stock of my gown. The damage wasn't great enough to be evident, but I had to take time to arrange my mussed hair and apply a cold towel to my eyes, for I'd been unable to restrain the tears as I fled from the scene of the attack.

Downstairs the music was playing. If I delayed too long, I'd be missed and Claude might be angry. I paused a moment before I left my rooms. Claude angry? It came to me then that he was probably responsible for all that had happened. It would have been like him to assign two of his employees to follow David and trap him.

I warned myself not to let this suspicion show, because that would only make matters worse. Whatever I did, whatever humiliation I now accepted, would be only because I'd be protecting David. When I thought I could face them, I made my way downstairs.

I passed the door to the dining room and I saw Laverne there with the two men on my card for this and the next dance. Their backs were toward me, but Laverne was apparently watching for me and he gave me a signal that all was well. If he only knew how everything had gone wrong.

I was relieved to see David on the bandstand, leading the orchestra, but I could also see that his evening clothes were soiled and when he turned to look out over the room, probably searching for me, I noted that the side of his face was swollen.

Someone behind me said, "Our maestro seems to have visited the punch bowl too freely during intermission."

"Perhaps his success has gone to his head," another voice echoed the idea that David had been imbibing too much. I hadn't counted on this, and it could damage David's reputation beyond repair if it was allowed to spread. There was nothing I could do about it here. I realized this might be the whole reason for the attack on him.

"Miss Stewart?" Someone spoke and I turned to find one of the men who had been with Laverne, now claiming what was left of the dance. I let him lead me to the floor and I made certain David would see me. He seemed relieved when he did, and turned back to face the orchestra, satisfied I was safe.

The rest of the evening was hazy, for I was too filled with fear and uncertainty to enjoy any part of it. I did notice that Walter hadn't been in evidence since intermission and I began to wonder if he'd been responsible for the assault on David. Claude spoke to me several times and gave no indication he knew about it.

At last the evening was over. I stood with Claude and Celina at the door, bidding those guests who would not stay what I hoped was a cordial good night. The people who did stay soon retired and the great house grew quiet.

The heat had wilted the flowers, the bunting looked the worse for wear. Outside, the Japanese lanterns had been extinguished. I hadn't seen David when he and the orchestra left, but they'd not have filed out with the departing guests anyway.

When Odette finally closed the door, Claude smiled at me. "It was an evening, wasn't it, my dear?"

"Yes," I agreed. "Thank you."

"I'm ready to drop," Celina said. "I'm going to bed. Please excuse me."

"I won't be long," Claude told her.

When she had disappeared up the stairs, I faced Claude. "May I speak with you now? It's very important."

"Why, of course. You seem upset, my dear."

"May we go to the library?" I had visions of Odette listening to every word if we talked here in the reception hall.

"Certainly." He took my elbow and we walked along the now empty drawing room. "It's amazing, Jana, how attractive this room was during the ball, and how forlorn it looks now. Nothing lasts, I'm afraid. But you were magnificent, I must say. You exceeded my expectations for being friendly and gracious."

I closed the library door and waited until he was seated behind his desk. "Mr. Duncan, it was not entirely a pleasant evening for me. I shall be frank about this, because I owe you the truth. I arranged with David Brennan to meet me at the summer house during intermission."

His face clouded. "I see."

"Mr. Duncan, I'm in love with David. We're going to be married."

"We'll go into that later. You mentioned an unpleasantness."

"Someone spied on us. David went to see who it was and two men—at least two—set upon him. You may have noticed his clothing was soiled and his face bruised."

"I didn't notice," he said. I thought he generously lied.

"I overheard someone say David must have been at the punch bowl too often. That's not true."

"And will you defend him by admitting you met him in the summer house?"

"Yes, if necessary. I'm not ashamed of it. But I would like to know who was responsible for that attack. I have little doubt but that it was arranged."

He smiled in that cold manner of his, reserved for the times when he was angry and tried not to show it. "Are you by any chance accusing me of arranging that?"

"I am accusing no one, but there has to be some answer to the reason for the attack."

"Sit down, Jana. I can see we need to talk this out. First of all, let me assure you that this is the first time I heard of the attack and I'm sorry it happened. I think I can account for it. This is a large estate and frequently people from nearby plantations will come here to spy or steal. Especially when there is an affair going on. I've had several of them chased away in the past. If David tried to reach them, no doubt they resisted so they might get away. They know I would have had them arrested if they'd been caught. Now that's over with, we shall get at the more important matters."

I felt drained of strength to fight this man, to argue the perfectly valid excuses he made. Claude Duncan was a clever man and therefore a dangerous one. I had to be careful.

"No doubt," I said, "you refer to my engagement to David Brennan."

"Engagement? Such things are not arranged in a summer house in the dead of night. I appreciate the fact that you may admire David. I do too. You are beholden to him for saving your life. But, my dear, admiration and gratitude are not love."

"It's far beyond gratitude," I insisted.

"Perhaps. But my advice is to be in no hurry."

"Why shouldn't I be, Mr. Duncan? When I'm in love with him. Why waste a moment of time without him when I am so in love?"

"I can see your point, Jana, and I appreciate it. However, we really don't know a great deal about David. He came here well recommended as a conductor, but that doesn't amount to a recommendation of his character. In fact, I know nothing about him."

"I do," I said. "I'm in love with him and to me nothing else matters."

"You know how much I want you to marry Walter?"

"Yes, I know."

"Walter's a fool for telling you too soon. You would have grown to like it here and to realize all of this could one day be yours."

"Mr. Duncan, I wish no part of it. I never came here with the idea of taking anything from you. I was desperate and you were kind enough to take me in because there was nowhere for me to go, with the exception of a pauper's jail. I was glad to work for you, to repay you in any way. . . ."

"I would not say I like the way," he broke in.

"I can't help that I fell in love with David, any more than I could help the awful events that made me destitute. If I am to remain here, I would prefer it on the basis of an employee."

"Don't be in such an all-fired rush," he said. "I'm asking you for an opportunity—a little time—to find out who David Brennan really it, and if he's worthy of a girl such as you. That's all I want. It should be a reasonable request and you ought to agree to it, even if you are so infatuated at the moment."

"It is not an infatuation, a thing of the moment," I insisted. "No matter what you discovered about David, it would make no difference. I'd still be in love with him and I would still refuse to marry your son under any circumstances."

"Now you're being nasty again."

"I am not. I am simply telling you how I feel. And I believe now that the best thing I can do is to leave Duncan House."

He leaned back. The moment of his victory had come, though I didn't realize it.

"Now, how can you do that? You'd only be returning to the same predicament I got you out of. They are strict in New Orleans about indigent people. The laws say you must be able to support yourself, or work will be found for you. Would you care to face that situation again?"

"David will see that I am cared for."

"David is not yet on salary and won't be for some time. The contracts are not even prepared, or terms worked out. I doubt the young man has enough to support you. As I understand it, he too lost almost everything in the sinking of the packet."

I was tired and close to tears. I didn't want to talk about this any more. I could readily understand what he meant. He was telling me, in that roundabout way of his, that should I leave him, I'd soon find myself back on the mercy of the probate judge who would have been instructed exactly what to do about my case. It seemed impossible to fight Claude Duncan.

"Sleep on it," he said cheerfully. "This is not a matter to be decided here and now. I'm sorry your evening was spoiled. Please believe that I had nothing to do with it."

I arose. "Thank you, Mr. Duncan," I said, and I left him rather abruptly. I went straight to my suite. When I opened the door, Laverne Cavet was seated in one of the parlor chairs. He arose at once.

"Close the door. This seemed the only way we could talk in safety. If you wish me to leave. . . ."

"Oh no," I said. "I just had a talk with Claude."

"An unsatisfactory one, by the look of you. Now what happened? I saw you come back from meeting David and I noticed you were . . . well, upset. I also saw that David looked as if he'd been in a fight."

"He was. Someone spied on us. David wanted to find out who it was and he found himself attacked by two men. We don't know who they were. He never even had a good look at them, nor did I."

"Claude is showing his hand, Jana."

"I believe so too. I have wondered where Walter was during all this."

"I happen to know, because I made it my business to find out. Walter went to bed just before intermission."

"Then that leaves Claude. Or those he paid to handle it."

"Seems so. Did he tell you his plans for you and Walter?"

"Yes, and I informed him I would never agree."

"Then it's all in the open now. I don't know if I'm sorry or pleased. It had to happen some time. What are you going to do?"

"I don't know. I suggested to Claude that I leave

here, but he pointed out that I'd be right back where I began—with nothing in view except being held as an indigent again."

"I will never allow that to happen, Jana. Not even if it costs me my friendship with Claude. I would advise against any hasty action, however."

"You are echoing Claude Duncan now."

"It is sound advice. Know where you stand—and where David stands—before you do anything drastic." He arose and tapped his lips to avoid a yawn. "For what it's worth now, I can tell you that you were tonight's belle of the ball. I never before heard so many compliments paid in one evening. And all deserved. I'll try to slip out of here without being seen."

"I'll make certain no one is in the corridor," I said. I opened the door to peer out. The corridor was deserted and darkened. Laverne tiptoed out of my suite and headed for his own rooms. I closed the door and felt as if the whole world had just dropped from beneath my feet. I had never been so confused in my life.

Nine

I prepared for bed in a numb sort of way, moving about, doing things automatically from habit alone. I blew out the last lamp and tried to settle down. Sleep was impossible, for my brain was too active to allow me to relax.

I sat up for several minutes. That didn't serve to make me drowsy and I felt trapped and beside myself with worry. I wanted to get out of here, to experience freedom if only for a little while. But half aware of what I was doing, I put on a walking dress and sturdy shoes. I threw a cape over my shoulders and quietly made my way downstairs. I unlocked the door, left it unlocked and closed it behind me. I began to walk. I didn't know what direction to take, so I walked straight ahead, away from the mansion.

I realized it would be dawn in a short time. The darkness should have frightened me, but it did not. I only felt a sense of release, being by myself. With an opportunity to think.

Claude could wreck whatever chance David had to succeed. I knew that. I also knew David would disregard such a threat, but I had to determine what was best for him. I appreciated Laverne's advice not to do anything rash. He was right. Besides, I would have to acquaint David with the facts which had developed. It would be his decision to make as much as mine.

I found that I was walking fast. I was already at the limits of the estate proper, though I could have continued walking for hours and still be on Claude's property. I crossed the dirt road to New Orleans. Soon now, farm drays and wagons would begin to move along this road bringing produce, milk and meat to the great city markets. At the moment it was dark and very quiet except for a multitude of night insects chirping and drumming away.

Suddenly I found myself facing the river. I looked back. The mansion wasn't even in sight. I'd walked a considerable distance. I didn't feel tired, but I realized it was a long way back. I paused before beginning the return walk to look at the river as its muddy water flowed by, lazily at this spot, because here the river was wide.

A hundred odd miles to the north my father and mother lay buried in the wreckage of the packet, or in the silt forming the bottom of this same river. The tragedy came back with a rush that made me cover my face and sob.

Our hopes and Papa's plans had been so high. In a moment's time everything had crashed, and now I found myself faced with a dilemma I felt I couldn't cope with.

I walked down to the river bank, standing on the very edge of it as if that brought me closer to the two people I'd loved so well. I bent my head in prayer for them.

Perhaps my sorrow and my state of mind made me less observant than usual. I had no warning, not even the scrape of a bush or the sound of a stealthy footfall, when I was seized from behind, lifted smoothly and swiftly, and thrown off the bank into the water.

I went under at once, dragged down by my already sodden dress and cloak. I did manage to get the cloak off and I surfaced to gasp for air. I twisted about to try and see who had thrown me into the water, but in the darkness all I could see was a vague shadow of someone who stood back from the bank.

I discovered the water here was deeper than I'd imagined, but at least I wasn't sinking into silt. I began to swim until I felt bottom under my feet.

Something splashed into the water close beside me. The next rock thrown from shore hit my shoulder a painful blow that sent me under again. I came up screaming in terror and at once another large stone landed in the water a few inches from my head. More followed. At least two struck me, though not seriously. I began to think about swimming away from shore, but my dress was dragging me down. I decided to make one more attempt to reach the bank. The shadowy form moved closer. The figure seemed extremely tall, a giant, until I realized he was holding a large rock high above his head. If he hit me with it, it would either kill me or send me unconscious to the bottom to drown.

Vaguely, I heard voices. They seemed to come from behind me. I raised my own voice in a scream. The man on the bank moved back. I heard the thud of the rock he'd been holding as it landed on the ground and then he was gone. I looked to my left and saw some sort of a boat, with a lantern in the prow, moving down the river. The men in it were chattering. Apparently they'd not heard my scream, for their voices remained level and unexcited, but they'd saved my life. The man who wished to murder me had given up just when I was all but doomed.

I crawled out of the water and I came upon the rock, so big that even a glancing blow with it would have likely resulted in my death. I sank to the ground to recover my wits. A slow, burning anger took possession of me and kept me from collapse.

This had been a deliberate attempt to kill me. The first one at the stone wall jump could have been the work of someone who hated the Duncans. I had conceded that, but this was not the work of any farmer or resentful employee of the Duncan empire. Someone had followed me here, thrown me into the river and then tried to stone me to death.

I had no idea who was responsible. All I did know was that every moment I spent at Duncan House was dangerous to me. For some unknown reason I was to be killed. I could no longer depend upon anyone at the house to safeguard me. I didn't know whom to trust.

Even Augusta, so mild and gentle a person, was too close to the family. So was Laverne, whom I had trusted implicitly. Walter was quite capable of this attempt. His father, as well, wasn't the type of man who'd hesitate at anything to get what he wanted. Except that Claude Duncan wanted me alive, to become the mother of his grandchild.

I began walking back to the mansion, stumbling along in the advancing dawn. There were lights on the first floor and I could hear activity around the stables where coachmen had bedded down and were now getting ready to harness their carriages and begin driving the overnight guests back.

I was soaked to the skin, slimy with mud. My hair was caked with it. I didn't want to be seen in this condition, so I went around to the back. There I found Coleen industriously sweeping the service porch. She gaped at me, the broom held just off the porch floor.

"I've had a mishap," I told her. "I shall need help in getting out of these wet things."

"Mum, I'll help all I can. Come along now. Nobody else is up yet. Cook's not awake, but she will be soon."

I made my way up the back stairs, Coleen went on ahead to make sure no one was abroad. She signaled me and I sped down the corridor to my suite. Coleen closed the door and locked it.

In the bathroom she assisted me in peeling off the dress and then my chemise. Nothing was worth saving, so we tossed it all into the bathtub temporarily.

I rinsed out my hair, while Coleen sped downstairs to fetch enough hot water for me to at least have a shallow bath. I also washed my hair of the silt. Coleen dried it with a large towel until it could be brushed into some kind of shape.

"How long were you downstairs?" I asked.

"Maybe half an hour before you came in. To tell you the truth, mum, I was hungry, being so busy last night

98

I didn't find the time to eat. So I came down for a bite and then I might as well begin cleaning up."

"Did you see anyone leave the house?"

"No, mum. I didn't even hear anybody stirring about."

"Did anyone return just before I did?"

"Not that I know of, mum."

"I will ask you to do me one more favor, Coleen. Please hurry to the stable and have the hostler harness a buggy and bring it around to the front immediately, before the guests begin leaving and the household awakens."

"Yes, mum, right away." Coleen rushed out of the suite. I dressed hastily, tied a scarf around my head because my hair was still damp. By the time I left the house, a buggy was waiting. The hostler helped me to board it. I slapped the reins smartly and began my trip to New Orleans. The first time alone.

On the way I calmed down some and tried to determine in my mind who could be responsible for that attempt on my life and, just as important—why. There were no answers. None my half-numbed mind could figure out. I found myself dozing part of the time, but the horse stayed on the road and as New Orleans really began to wake up, I reached the outskirts.

I already knew that David was living at one of the lesser hotels and I went there, finding my way easily enough. I tied the horse, entered the hotel and asked for David. A porter told me he was in the dining room.

I found him alone at a table near the rear of the restaurant. He was so startled he wasn't sure he recognized me at first. Then he jumped to his feet and came to meet me.

"What brings you here at this hour, Jana? You must have left Duncan House at dawn."

"I had to see you. It wouldn't wait. Can we talk here?"

He seated me and called over a waiter to order a

substantial breakfast for me, guessing that I'd not taken time to eat before I set out for the city.

The strong New Orleans coffee stimulated me and banished some of my fatigue. I first related my narrow escape from drowning only this same morning.

David was aghast at the attempt. "Tried to stone you after throwing you into the river? What's behind this? What have you done to deserve this?"

"I defied Claude last night, if that has any meaning," I said.

"Tell me about it, Jana."

"Claude advised me not to marry you. He wants grandchildren and I am to be their mother."

"Walter? He actually wants you to marry Walter?"

"I was aware of that before."

"Yes, I know. But it sounded too fantastic to believe."

"He hinted that, unless I abandoned plans to marry you, he'd destroy your career here. You'd not be retained to conduct the French Opera."

"I'm willing to accept that," David said. "I'll sacrifice anything, but I won't let you go."

"What can we do, David? It means you'll have to begin over again. Look for another city in which to conduct. Do you have the means to get along until you find other work?"

"I've very little. I came here with my expenses paid, but if I'm not placed under contract, I certainly won't be rolling in wealth. Any ready cash I had went down with the packet."

"Do you see a way out of this?" I asked.

"Yes. Marry me now. We'll get along somehow."

"Claude has hinted that if I leave Duncan House, I may find myself jailed as an indigent."

"If you marry me they can't hold you."

"I don't know, David. I'm afraid this might hurt you too much."

"It won't hurt me a fraction as much as if you leave me and marry Walter."

"I would die if that happened."

"It won't. Be sure of that. What worries me most is that attempt on your life."

"It wasn't the first one. I was also thrown, because someone ambushed my horse at a stone wall jump."

"Let's consider these problems one at a time," he suggested. "And eat your bacon and eggs, darling. You can't starve yourself at this stage. Now—there's Laverne Cavet. All I know about him is that he is a trader of some sort, unmarried, lives alone, he's wealthy and has been a friend of Claude's for a long time."

"He's been kind and understanding," I said. "He told me that Claude is wrong in this desire for a grandson. No matter what happens, he would not stand to gain anything from my death. I can't see how we can suspect him."

"Good. I feel the same way. He has championed me all the way. What of Mrs. Duncan's sister?"

"Augusta? Such a kindly, simple person, David. She would be incapable of even scheming a thing like murder."

"For a moment let's go back to the ball. When you met me and I was batted on the head. When you returned to the house, was anybody missing?"

"Laverne was in the dining room, wining the two men who had the first dances with me after intermission. That was to give me time enough to be with you. Laverne did not leave the house. Nor did Claude. Walter had disappeared though. I was later told he'd gone to bed."

"Do you know for certain that he did?"

"No, I do not. Except I believe the man who told me he'd gone to bed."

"Laverne?"

"Yes. Moreover, I find it hard to believe Walter has even the ambition to try to kill me. Besides, he has every reason to wish me alive. I don't think he cares whether or not he marries me, but he wants to obey his father. So what would be the point of killing me?"

"The same goes for Claude," David mused. "He too

101

wants and needs you alive. Can it be someone on the outside?"

"I'm practically a stranger here. I've had no outside contacts until last night. We're not getting anywhere, darling."

"There's Celina, Mrs. Claude Duncan."

I waited until my coffee cup was refilled and the waiter out of earshot. "She is a determined woman," I admitted. "And as ruthless as her husband. Perhaps even more so. But Celina is not strong enough to throw me into the river, nor to lift above her head the heavy rock which the murderer was about to throw at me just before that yawl came along to frighten him off."

"She could pay someone to do this for her. It's not hard to find a man who'll cheerfully commit murder if there's enough in it for him."

"True. But again, wouldn't she want me alive too? So I might bring grandchildren into the house?"

"The only one left," David said resignedly, "is Marie, Walter's wife."

"I've thought about her too," I said. "Nobody seems to know what really happened to her. They don't even like to talk about her at the house. From what I can learn, they must have discouraged her enough that she left. Claude would be good at that, but Celina might outdo him in making the poor girl uncomfortable."

"What did happen to her? She was a New Orleans girl, she had relatives here. Why didn't she return to them? Where did she go, to vanish so thoroughly? Even if she was so dismayed with the Duncans and wanted to get far away from them, she could at least have written a letter to her own folks."

"We don't know but that she did," I said.

"True. I'm going to look them up and find out."

"She took little or nothing with her," I said. "I'm wearing her clothes and there are a great number of gowns and shoes . . . everything. She was a fine judge

102

of clothes and style, so why didn't she take some of her things when she disappeared?"

"The missing Marie seems to be suddenly important," David said. "I'll see what I can do about finding her. This is a good day for it. There's no performance tonight. Tomorrow night is an important one, so I'll have to spend the day rehearsing, I'm afraid. Will you stay and help me?"

"I must go back. Claude is angry enough now. I don't want him to take out his anger on you."

"You may be returning to more danger," he objected.

"I'm forewarned now and I intend to be very careful. I wanted you to know what was going on, especially about Claude's insistence that I marry his son."

"But Marie isn't dead. He can't prove she is. How can Walter get married again?"

"As Walter said, his father can fix it."

"No doubt. Again, I wish you wouldn't go back."

"I'd like nothing better than to stay here with you. I'd feel safe then, but I owe them something. Besides, I have a notion that if this strange mystery is to be solved, it will be done at Duncan House and not in New Orleans. I feel better now. You are warned and I'm prepared to face the Duncans. Thank you for breakfast. I'll do my best to get in the city again to hear you direct."

"Tomorrow night would be a good time," he suggested. "I'll see you to your buggy."

Ten

When I returned to Duncan House, I went straight to my suite, fortunate in not encountering anyone. I was too tired to do more than get into bed and sleep for five hours. It was Coleen who awakened me, at orders from Celina.

"They think you're sick," she said. "They were worried about you."

"I'm not sick," I told her. "I feel fine now. I was up all night. Will you see that I am served something to eat. And thank you, Coleen."

She hurried away to see about the food. I attended to my hair, dressed and went downstairs. A place had been set for me at the dining table, though it was mid-afternoon.

As I buttered warm rolls and drank coffee, Claude came in and sat down beside me. "What did your young man think about the situation?" he asked.

He must have people reporting to him about everything that goes on in New Orleans, I thought. "He doesn't like it, Mr. Duncan."

"No, I suppose he doesn't. Did you come to any decision?"

"I don't know what you mean."

"Like marrying him immediately?"

"No, we talked about it, but we made no decision."

"You're an unusual girl, Jana. You could have lied to me, but I know you're telling the truth."

"I do not lie, Mr. Duncan. Now I am going to ask you a question and I hope that you do not lie to me.

You know about the trap set for me behind that stone fence?"

"Yes, of course."

"Were you responsible for that?"

"I?" he exclaimed. "I don't want you hurt in any way."

"Very early this morning, just before dawn, I found myself unable to sleep, so I took a walk. It was a random walk. I paid little attention to where I was going and I found myself at the bank of the river. While I stood there, someone rushed up behind me, lifted me from my feet and threw me into the water."

"Good heavens! Who was it?"

"I couldn't tell. That isn't all. When I tried to climb onto the bank, this person threw rocks at me. I have a badly bruised shoulder from one of them. Finally he was about to use a great big piece of stone which would have surely killed me, or sent me to the bottom unconscious to drown. A yawl came down the river and frightened him away, otherwise I'm sure I would now be dead."

As I spoke I could see how agitated Claude became. His face showed an expression of surprise and horror, which could not be faked. In my opinion he had known nothing about this.

"Do you think I did that?" he asked.

"Someone did."

"It was not my work, Jana." He half arose, pushed his chair closer to mine. "I want you to marry my son so I may have a grandson. I want him to be strong and healthy. I want you to care for him, bring him up and make a man of him. Not the kind of a man my son is, but a real man. I would give my life for that. Would I, now, try to harm you? By killing you, I would destroy the only good chance I have of getting a grandson."

"There are other girls who might think they were getting a bargain," I said. "Why me? I meant to ask you that before."

106

"It's simple. I knew your father and mother. I know about their parents. I know you are descended from a fine strain. Good bloodlines. Everything I would want for the mother of my grandson. Don't you see? Nobody else will do."

"I'm sorry," I said.

"So am I. Your young man could go far with my help."

"Which means you will see to it he does not get the contract?"

"Let us say, I won't offer to help him get it. I can't control the Board of Directors that will appoint him."

That, I thought, was his first lie. I did believe him when he claimed no knowledge of the attack on me at the river's edge. The committee for the French Opera would do exactly what he said, or take their cue from him if he said nothing. I began to lose hope.

"Tomorrow evening," Claude said, "a new opera premières at the French Opera House and David Brennan is to lead the orchestra. It's a most important assignment. If he does well with it, I cannot see how anyone could influence the committee against him. Would you care to be my guest at the performance?"

It was unexpected and generous, I thought. "Yes, very much. I'm pleased that you asked me."

"The ladies are still too tired after the ball to attend, so there will be only you and I and Laverne. I haven't even asked Walter. The only thing he enjoys at the opera is the opportunity to sleep."

"Thank you. All David needs is a chance to show how great he is. This will be it. And you'll be proud of him, Mr. Duncan."

"I hope so. We'll let matters rest until then, shall we?"

"Yes. Yes, of course we will."

He frowned. "I'm worried about these strange attempts on your life. I can't see any reason for them."

"Nor can I. They puzzle me as much as they do you.

So far as I know, nobody would gain a thing at my death."

"True enough. You did say your father was carrying a large sum of money on him when the packet caught fire and blew up?"

"Yes sir. Everything he had was converted into cash and he carried it in a money belt."

"I wonder . . . could it be . . . this has something to do with all that money?"

"Mr. Duncan, my father and mother shared a cabin almost adjacent to the boiler deck. When it blew up so did barrels of gun powder and the boilers themselves. That was the part of the ship which suffered the most damage. There was practically nothing left."

"Then that idea seems worthless. I want you to be very careful. Try not to wander about alone. If you feel you need to take the air, let me know and I, or Laverne, will accompany you."

"I don't like to impose," I said, "but I do believe it's a worthy precaution."

"We'll find some arrangement we both agree on," he said. "You are an unusually sensible girl. So we'll bide our time for the moment."

He left me to finish my meal and he also left me wondering exactly what kind of a man he was. He'd threatened before with imprisonment as an indigent; now he was compromising, giving me time to decide, even offering to let me share in David's success.

I was at loose ends now. With the ball over, Duncan House suddenly seemed too quiet. There was nothing for me to do. I knew that Celina customarily took a long nap about this time. I had no idea where Laverne was and I didn't care where Walter happened to be. That left Augusta, and I decided to pay her a visit, for she spent much of her time in her two-room suite.

She called to me to enter when I knocked and I found her engaged in delicate petite-point work, wearing brass-rimmed glasses through which she peered at the fine stitches, then at me, until she touched her glasses and laughed.

"I do forget I'm wearing them and the world is actually a big enough place that I can see well, but this work is so fine. . . ."

"It's beautiful." I appraised the chair cover she was making. "I've never learned that skill."

"Don't," she advised, "and save your eyesight. Did you enjoy the ball?"

"Oh yes. It was a wonderful affair."

"You were certainly the center of attention, Jana. You made quite a hit."

"I'm glad. Thank you for telling me."

"Claude is giving you a great deal of trouble, isn't he?"

"You know about that?" I sat down close by her. She bent over her work, talking as she created those tiny stitches.

"I have so little to do, I keep track of everything," she said with a soft laugh. "Mostly I don't say much, but I know what's going on." Now she did look up, directly at me, over the glasses which had slipped down along her nose. "Don't let them hurt you, dear child. Don't give in to them. Walter is a horrible excuse for a man. Even his father cannot tolerate him. Poor Marie cursed the day she married him."

"I didn't know about that," I said.

"Oh yes. But one can't feel too sorry for her. She was a lovely girl to be sure, but she married Walter for his money. Or rather, his father's money. Perhaps it would have worked out, but when she discovered she could not have children, she ceased to exist so far as Claude was concerned."

"What do you think happened to her, Augusta?"

"Oh, I don't know. Nobody does. She was a temperamental sort of girl. I suspect she grew tired of the whole thing and packed up and left."

"She left," I said. "But she didn't pack up. Everything

she owned is still here. I know, because it was turned over to me to use."

This time Augusta laid her work aside and removed the glasses. "Yes . . . she did leave us abruptly. Perhaps she found someone she liked better than Walter. Not a difficult thing to do, Walter being what he is. Lazy, treacherous, a profound liar. He can be cruel, even brutal."

"I've informed Mr. Duncan that I will not marry Walter."

"I know that too. But you will, my dear. He'll make you. I don't know how, but Claude always finds a way. He can be as cruel as his son. More so, because his cruelty reaches you in subtle ways that last."

"What should I do?"

"I would go to my room, pack what belonged to me, or was given me, have one of the stable hands drive me to New Orleans and never come back."

"I can't do that."

"I know. I should have done it years ago, but I didn't. Now I make the best of it. Thank heavens, I'm not married to a man like Walter."

"Augusta, do you know of any reason why someone would wish to kill me?"

"Good heavens, child, of course I don't. Who could possibly dislike you that much?"

"I'm afraid there are more reasons than simple dislike," I said. "It could be fear, because I know something, the significance of which I have not yet discovered. Or I may be in someone's way. I don't know the reason. I only know that twice I was close to being killed. That's why I asked about Marie. I wonder if she could have had something to do with it."

Augusta's eyes were wide in surprise. "But she isn't even here."

"I don't mean that Marie personally was responsible for those two attempts on my life, but her presence here before I came, her disappearance, perhaps one of those has set the stage for the danger that seems to come upon me."

"I don't see how," Augusta said. "She just . . . just vanished. Of her own accord, certainly."

"Didn't anyone try to find her? I mean really search?"

"We thought she'd come back, Jana. Honestly, we genuinely believed that, and by the time she was gone for weeks, it didn't seem to make any difference. We were, frankly, glad to be rid of her. She was a trial to all of us."

"But it does seem as if someone would attempt to find her."

"Oh, I suppose her parents did. They live in New Orleans. They came here and tried to get money out of Claude, saying that Walter was to blame for her running away. Needless to say, they didn't get a penny, which was no more than they deserved."

"Wasn't Walter interested enough to find her?"

"Oh, he did some crying about it. I guess he was sorry she left him. Maybe his pride was hurt, but he soon forgot about her."

"I wish she'd come back," I said. "That would solve the problem for David and me."

"If she did return, I think Claude would pay her to go away again. He's already beginning steps to have her declared legally dead. It will take some doing, because the law says seven years, and she's been missing . . . let me see now . . . well, I do declare . . . it was a year ago. All that time. Seems like yesterday."

I shook my head sadly. Only a year ago and she would now be declared dead. Money and power accomplished almost anything in New Orleans. Augusta picked up her sewing again, so I left her and went downstairs. I was restless. Being confined to the house bored me. I wanted to go out, at least for a short walk. I knew it could be dangerous, so I looked for either Laverne or Claude, but I was unable to find either.

Odette, inspecting the newly reassembled drawing room,

111

didn't look up as I entered. I didn't intend to allow her to intimidate me with this sort of silence.

"Have you seen Mr. Duncan or Mr. Cavet?" I asked.

"Both of 'em went down to the plantation proper. Won't be back 'till sundown."

I said, "Thank you," and turned away, but on second thought I faced her again. "Odette, you have been barely civil to me ever since I came here. I have not knowingly caused you any harm, nor slighted you in any way. Why do you dislike me so?"

"You'd be better off if you just left. Like the other one did."

"Marie? What do you know about her disappearance?"

Odette carefully folded the dust cloth she invariably carried about with her. She picked up the feather duster and flicked it at one of the chairs nearby. "Don't know anything about where she went. I had nothing to do with it."

"Do you think she's alive?" I asked.

Her face grew pale as her thin mouth grew even thinner. "Why do you say that, eh? What right have you to say such a thing?"

"Every right, I should say." Suddenly I began to see behind the reason for her hatred of me. It was a guess, but one worth following. "It might be that Walter was responsible. . . ."

"You keep your mouth shut!" She half screamed at me. "Walter didn't have anything to do with her running off. Don't you go blaming him. She used to call him a fool. I slapped her once for that—and she knew I was right in hitting her too, because she never went to Mr. Duncan about it. No sir, she took it because she deserved it and now you . . . you come here and say Walter killed her. . . ."

"Then you do think Marie is dead?" I persisted.

"I never said so. I don't know if she's dead or alive. I'm only glad she's out of here and she's stopped tan-

112

talizing poor Walter like he was a nine-year-old. I hated her. I don't care if she's never found."

"It's Walter you're protecting," I said. My guess had been right. "Odette, I mean Walter no harm. I haven't called him names, nor ridiculed him, even though I should have after the tricks he played on me. The only thing I know about him is that I will not marry him as Mr. Duncan seems to think I will."

"Walter, he don't want you. He told me that. I know what he wants and it ain't you, my fancy miss. Best thing you can do is go away."

"If only it was as easy as that," I said.

"You shouldn't have come to him for help."

"Odette, I didn't know the man. I'd lost my parents and everything we had. The authorities wanted to know if I had any friends or relatives and I answered truthfully. Did you wish me to lie about it?"

"Best thing you could have done—best for all of us. Walter, you, and the rest of 'em."

"Good afternoon, Odette," I said.

I walked out of the house, against Claude's wishes, but I was angry and somewhat puzzled. I wanted to think, to be alone. A walk around the estate would give me a chance to try and solve this fresh problem. I realized there might be danger, so I made up my mind not to drift far away, but to remain as close to the house and the workers' cabins as possible. If there were people about, the risk of being attacked would be less. Where the working people lived, there were scores of people about. Women and children abounded. I had often heard the children at noisy play.

I entered the dirt road between the cabins. Instantly the noise stopped. The children stared at me, the women darted inside their cabins. One little girl, brown as a nut, timidly approached me. I held out my hands to her. She gave a happy little cry and ran to me. I hugged her tightly before I set her down.

"What a pretty little girl you are," I said. "I'm glad you're not afraid of me."

"Mama says folks from the big house come, we got to get out of the way," she said.

"Now that's all wrong. Just because we live in the big house doesn't mean I don't like children. Whatever gave you that idea?"

I asked the question loudly, for I knew the mothers were listening. About a dozen emerged from the cabins. Most of the others, I learned later, were at work in the fields. The slim, attractive woman who claimed the little girl by placing a hand on her shoulder, managed a frightened smile.

"Pleased you came down, ma'am."

"I should have come down much sooner," I said. "From now on I will. I can perhaps teach the children new games . . . things to do. For me to do as well."

"Pleased you come down any time, ma'am."

"Have you been ordered to stay away from us?" I asked.

"No, ma'am. We're treated fine."

"Then why did the children run away and why did you not remain outside to greet me?"

"It was that other one. She didn't like us."

"Other one? Do you mean the woman who was married to Walter and who disappeared?"

"Yes'm. That's the one. She used to come screaming that there was too much noise. I reckon she didn't like kids. I can see you do, ma'am."

"I love them," I said. "They all seem to be so well cared for. I'm going to enjoy visiting them."

Here I was, looking into the future, when I only wished to get away from this place. But there'd be a few days, I hoped, when I could come down to the quarter and enjoy the children. Other mothers joined us, and for a while we talked and visited joyfully. When I left them, I felt in a far better frame of mind. I meant to see if I could find some toys. If not, perhaps we could make some.

I walked the length of the long row of cabins. I felt perfectly secure here, for there were so many people about. At the end of the street I saw a grove of tall, weathered oaks in the distance. It was a stand of trees in the middle of the otherwise planted ground. I thought there must be a reason for this, so I wandered over there and discovered I was in the midst of a cemetery.

I knew that burials were all in tombs, for the moisture beneath the soil didn't permit ordinary burials. I'd already seen that New Orleans had a number of these graves above the ground. Some were very elaborate, others quite plain, but they formed what seemed to be entire cities.

This one was smaller and I realized it must be for the use of the family and probably the plantation workers. There were four large tombs decorated with angels, their cement doors closed and guarded by iron filigreed gates.

There was also a long wall, honeycombed with open niches among the closed ones. Each sealed tomb bore a slab engraved with the name of the deceased, birth and death dates. I wondered how many of these were occupied by people who'd been slaves.

I examined the larger tombs. The Duncans had lived here a long time, for each tomb contained several crypts. Some were dated fifty years ago. I could understand why Claude Duncan wanted the family name perpetuated, but it wasn't going to be by my children.

Eleven

I left the cemetery, skirted the far end of the row of cabins and entered a wide field of lush grass, cropped short. I felt perfectly safe here, because there was nowhere someone might lay in wait for me and then spring out to attack. The grass was soft and springy underfoot and I seemed surrounded by a peaceful kind of silence.

My thoughts returned to my wonderful days in St. Louis with Mama and Papa. They'd been so filled with joy and such promise for the future. Then one steamboat captain's greed for fame, and the carelessness of his crew, had changed everything.

Had it not been for my meeting David, I should have been utterly lost by now. In him I found the stamina to endure the sorrow of my loss, and then to face these strange, unexplained dangers which threatened me.

This wide open area was bounded on three sides by forest, some of it heavily grown, other sections were sparse. Further on was the section of pasture where I'd ridden with Walter. Therefore, when I saw a horseman emerge from one of the riding paths, I wasn't alarmed. Walter had a tendency to slouch in the saddle and was easy to recognize. I didn't like him, he was full of senseless tricks, sometimes even perilous, but Walter offered no other threat than that, because he wanted to marry me and therefore would be more apt to protect than harm me.

He rode sedately until he was about halfway across the cleared area. Then he gave the yell of a wild man, spurred his horse and came racing toward me as fast as the stallion could go.

I believed he was showing off. I stopped and waited for him, thinking, one day he'll break his neck. . . . He wasn't going to stop! I suddenly realized that, and he wasn't going to slow down nor swerve past me. He was doing his best to actually run me down.

I leaped to one side, barely in time. Walter pulled up, turned the horse quickly and came toward me again. Once more I ran as fast as I could, and when I heard the sound of the hoofbeats very close behind, I veered to one side. Each time the stallion went on by and Walter reined up, turned so fast his horse reared, and started after me again.

I'd kept on more or less of a straight line toward the heavy forest border on this cleared area. Once there, I'd be reasonably safe, but my chances of making it seemed slim. I took no time to wonder why Walter was doing his best to kill me, I only knew that he was, and my life depended upon avoiding his onrushing horse.

I veered again, narrowly avoiding being brought down by the horse. I was getting closer to the forest now and some measure of hope began to arise within me. From here on, I couldn't afford to veer off, but I must make the forest in one straight run. That meant calling upon the last of my reserves. I actually did force myself to run faster. Walter had turned the horse and was using a quirt to gain speed so he might overtake me.

I thought I was going to make it and in my mind was the wild hope that, if I did, Walter wouldn't be able to pull up his horse fast enough to avoid crashing into the thickness of the forest. That was when I risked a look over my shoulder to see how much time I had. My foot struck something, possibly a stone. It didn't matter, for the result was that I fell headlong and skidded along the grass from the impetus of my mad speed.

I tried to get up. It was useless. Rider and horse were almost upon me. I was going to be killed. There wasn't a chance left for me to survive. That horse would trample me to death in half a minute.

118

I saw the froth coating the mouth of the animal, saw the wild reddened eyes, saw the front legs come up as the horse reared—and then the hoofs came down, but a yard from where I was crouched. Walter lay over the saddle horn and laughed until the tears rolled down his face.

I got up quickly, and with little attention to dignity, I strode over to stand beside the quivering horse.

"I'm going to your father about this," I said. "You just must be insane."

His laughter ceased and he leaned down to address me in a cold, intense voice. "You pack up and get out of here. We don't want you here. Go away and don't come back. If you won't do that, next time I *will* ride you down."

I backed away two small steps, startled by the venom in his voice. "Why?" I demanded. "Tell me why!"

"You just go away, that's all."

"Your father says I must marry you. What do you say to that?"

"I won't do it. I won't marry you. That's why you've got to go, before Papa has his way. All I want is for people to let me alone. That's all I want, to be let alone."

I said, "Walter, get down off that horse if you wish to continue talking to me."

"Don't want to talk any more."

"Yes, you do. Because I know the reason you want me to go away."

He swung out of the saddle and walked up to face me. "You do? You know why?"

"You're still in love with Marie," I said.

"Who told you that?" He half screamed, for his sudden rage was making him lose control of himself. I was afraid he was going to become violent. I had to calm him down. This man was unpredictable, therefore dangerous.

"It's right that you should be in love with her," I said. "I'm on your side."

His rage disappeared as rapidly as it had arisen. "You mean that, Jana?"

"You wouldn't have married her if you were not in love with her. And she wouldn't have married you, if she hadn't known you would care for her and love her."

"Nobody else ever understood. . . ."

"You didn't want her to go away."

"But she did leave. She said she couldn't stand living with me."

"Are you sure that's what she said?" I asked, still desperately trying to mollify him and keep him calm. "Or did she tell you she couldn't stand living here any more?"

"I don't know. I thought she meant me." He was growing uncertain and easier to handle.

"Walter, when your father decided Marie was a liability rather than the potential mother of his grandchild, he didn't want her any more and made himself clear on that subject. It was he she ran from, not you."

"Do you think that? Honest?" he asked, begging for an affirmative reply.

"It seems quite clear this is so. Did she say anything else before she left?"

"No, nothing."

"Did you know she was leaving?"

"No. I'd have tried to stop her. . . ."

"She just walked out? By herself?"

"I don't know. I wasn't here. Papa sent me to his city office on business. I was gone all afternoon and when I came back she was gone. I didn't even know it then. Not until I went to bed and looked for her. I searched the whole house . . . she was gone."

"She left no message, no note?"

"Nothing. She just left."

"Did she take anything with her? Money, jewels, extra clothes?"

"She just opened the door and walked out. That's the way it looked to me."

"You never heard a word from her again?"

"Never."

"Walter, did you try to find her? Did you search, ask questions, talk to her folks?"

"Her folks wouldn't let me in the house. They said I was to blame. I looked all around the plantation. I thought she might have had an accident. I didn't ask anybody to help me, because I was ashamed. When a woman leaves a husband it's always his fault, not hers."

"Those times—trying to make my horse throw me, the dead tree branch at the jump, giving me that wild ride the day we went into the city for the opera . . . all those things were meant to frighten me so I'd leave. Isn't that true?"

"Yes . . . not the branch at the stone wall, though. I never put that there. You can't say I did that."

"All right, I'll take your word for it. The other things were to drive me away so I wouldn't marry you after your father said he was going to have Marie declared dead."

"Yes. I asked him not to do this. I wanted him to wait. Marie's coming back. I know she is. She didn't hate me. If she wanted to come back, I'd offer to live with her in the city, not here on the plantation. I'd go to work and I'd have nothing more to do with Papa. I hate him. I hate Mama too, because she wants the same thing he does. Who cares if the Duncan name keeps on going? Not me. Far as I'm concerned it can die with me and good riddance."

"Do you know of any reason why my death would benefit anyone?" I asked.

"I didn't want to kill you," he said hastily. "I swear I didn't. I could have, but I don't hate you that way. If you'd just leave here. . . ."

"I didn't ask if you tried to kill me. I meant is there someone else who might wish me dead?"

He shook his head ponderously from side to side. "I don't know. What good would it be killing you?"

"I wish I knew, Walter."

"You going to tell Papa what I did?" There was an element of worry in his voice now.

"Not if you'll promise me you'll never try anything like this again."

"I promise. It was a fool thing. I do lots of fool things, but I won't hurt you. Never!"

"Then I'll say nothing. We will, however, agree on one thing. You will not marry me and I shall never marry you."

"I sure say amen to that. I just want Marie to come back. Do you think she will, Jana?"

"I don't know. I never knew Marie, but they say she was very beautiful."

He closed his eyes as if to summon up her image. "She was. Oh, she was so beautiful, she'd take your breath away. I never thought she'd marry me. But she did. That shows she must have been in love with me."

"Of course she was." Inwardly I wondered how a man with a reputation as a chaser and a gambler could possibly be this naïve. It came to me then that his reputation as a rogue was built on sand. Actually, Walter was slow in thought and deed. His reputation as a gambler must have been established because he lost so consistently. His true nature and intellect were barely hidden under a thin veil of sophistication that he had somehow acquired. He was a man not to fear but to feel sorry for.

"I will say nothing about the way you tried to frighten me," I promised once more.

He nodded, swung back into the saddle and rode away. Still shaking, I began walking back to the mansion, now certain it wasn't safe for me to step outdoors. I felt sure that Walter was not responsible for all the other things that had happened to me—but who *was*, then?

I had made up my mind that the one way to put a stop to Claude Duncan's insistence on maintaining the Duncan family line was to bring Marie back. It would be much harder for Claude to force a divorce than the legal presumption of death. Walter would defy him if it came to a divorce and probably Claude knew or sensed this.

The remainder of the day was quiet and boring. Odette kept out of my way. Whether on purpose or not, I didn't know. Augusta apparently still worked on her petite-point, and Celina must have decided to spend the day in bed—which she sometimes did—for I never saw her all day.

Both Claude and Laverne were at the New Orleans office of the plantation, so I was left on my own. I read and passed some of the time in examining the possessions Marie had left behind for any possible clues as to her disappearance. I discovered nothing. My spirits were buoyed by the knowledge that tomorrow night I was to attend the theatre and see David conduct a première performance of a new opera. This was a most important assignment. I knew he'd been rehearsing for several days and I prayed he would prove himself once and for all time, so he would be granted the contract he sought.

Next day, my spirits were even happier, for it was now but a short time before I'd see David. There was no change in Claude's plans. He and I, and Laverne, would attend. Celina didn't feel up to it and Augusta gave no reason, simply stated she wished to remain at home.

Early that morning Claude decided to go to the city and Laverne and I would meet him at the hotel for supper before we went to the opera. At mid-afternoon, I was ready and impatient, while Laverne was still dessing. Finally we were on our way in one of the carriages.

I had always believed I could trust Laverne. Whatever I'd told him in confidence so far had never reached Claude's ears. The more I'd mulled over Walter's strange behavior and his reasons for it, the more I wondered about it. I wanted the opinion of someone else, not in-fluenced because of blood ties.

Laverne heard me out. I told him how Walter had tried to frighten me away, culminating in what had seemed a savage attempt to kill me by riding me down.

"Walter," Laverne said, "often seems to be two people. I've seen him in a card game showing more courage at bluffing, and more good judgment of cards and people that you'd give him credit for. He also used to be one who'd seek female company and if the lady had to be pursued and persuaded, so much the better. At such times, he could be suave, the perfect gentleman. Then again, he enjoys fool stunts like those he worked on you. I've seen him vicious enough to kill someone and meek enough to kneel. I don't know what to make of him. He puzzles his father as well."

"Which part of him predominates and governs his secret thoughts?" I asked.

"How would I know? One thing he said I will dispute. He claims to have been in love with Marie and wants her back. That is a lie. He hated her because she nagged him, reminded him constantly of the fact that he didn't provide for her, but left that to his father. When Claude proved niggardly in giving her money, she turned on Walter harder than ever and ordered him to get her more. Which she knew was an impossibility, unless Walter went to work—a fate Walter avoided as if it were lethal."

"Did she run away because she hated Walter the most? Or Walter's father even more?"

"She hated Claude passionately, because when he discovered she would not provide grandchildren, he barely acknowledged that she existed. Walter, on the other hand, endured her nagging because he thought she was entitled to more than Claude was willing to grant. Let's say, she didn't like either one of them."

I was silent for a while, contenting myself with pondering what Laverne had just told me, and looking at the smaller plantations we passed, waving to field workers at times and keeping my handkerchief against my nose to prevent any more breathing in of the red dust that formed a cloud every time a horse's hoof struck the road.

"Do you think Mr. Duncan will somehow force me to marry Walter?" I asked.

124

"I'm afraid so, my dear."

"I don't think he can do it with all his money and his power. He can't stop David and me from being in love."

"Quite true," Laverne admitted, "but he may be able to capitalize even on that fact. He is a shrewd man who is accustomed to search for loopholes that give him an edge in all of his dealings. I have seen him backed into a corner by his enemies, without a chance to escape. Or so it seemed. But he always got away, by using his wits. Under no circumstances regard him as a vulnerable man."

Laverne's lecture was well meant, but it served to dishearten me considerably. I wished I could have arranged to see David before the opera, but that was impossible. There'd only be time to meet Claude, have our supper and reach the theatre in time.

Claude had arranged for a table and we were led to it most deferentially by the head waiter. Claude arrived fifteen minutes later, looking like a man harried by business commitments.

"Well," he said, "it ought to be a great evening. Everyone is determined this shall be a night to remember, when a new opera is born and New Orleans gets a better place on the map because of it."

"Did you see David?" I asked.

"Oh yes—for about half an hour. I listened to part of the overture. It's good. It's very good. David will earn his contract tonight and probably, if he asks," Claude gave me a slow wink, "his salary may be even more than has already been offered him."

"I'm going to be frank, Claude," Laverne said. "You keep insisting that Jana marry Walter, though you know she is in love with David. Yet you keep promoting David, now to a position where he easily can afford to marry her. Your intentions and your actions appear to conflict."

"Perhaps they do," Claude replied cheerfully. He was drinking his whiskey like a man who felt he needed its lift. "I try to be fair. In this case I hold no brief against

David for being in love with Jana. One day, they may even find themselves able to marry."

"How can you say such a thing?" I asked indignantly.

"Oh yes, you and David can marry some day. But not until you have provided me with a grandson, preferably. I will even settle for a granddaughter, though she would be somewhat a disappointment."

Laverne gave a short, harsh laugh. "Why? If you took control of her, as you certainly will, you'd turn her into your own image and make her more of a man than a woman. There are times, Claude, when I don't like you. This is one of them."

"You see," Claude laughed loudly and called for more drinks. "I let my friends say what they like. I enjoy people being frank with me, but they have to endure what I say also. Laverne, for instance, has never married. He has been escort to many, many desirable girls and women, but until now, I don't believe marriage ever entered his head."

"Until he met you, my dear Jana. But he knows how end to this conversation by bringing it to a head promptly.

"Until he met you, my dear Jana. But he knows how unavailable you are. I insist you marry my son, you insist upon marrying David, so that leaves poor Laverne a bad third. Now, am I correct?"

He addressed the question to Laverne whose face had first turned pinkish with embarrassment, and was now being transformed into a fiery red from rage that threatened to overpower his better judgment. He must have caught himself just in time, for he settled back and finished his drink.

"My dear Claude," he said, "what I should do now is slap your face and send my seconds to you. But inasmuch as we are old friends and neither of us know one end of a rapier from another, and we are notoriously bad shots, we might harm one another in a duel. Therefore, I shall disregard what you say by merely calling you a madman."

126

Claude reacted, as I knew he would, with a loud burst of laughter. Because of Laverne's comments I couldn't restrain laughing myself and Laverne gladly joined in. But this was something I'd never before realized. I had looked upon Laverne as someone who might take Papa's place, not as a possible suitor . . . a man who might look at David as a rival.

Twelve

The lines of ticket purchasers had disappeared by the time we reached the French Opera House, but there was still a press of people waiting to get in and the sidewalk was busy with the dancers, singers and roaming musicians trying to earn a few picayunes.

A way was quickly cleared for us and we passed through the crowded lobby and were led to Claude's stall. The orchestra was already tuning up, and ten minutes after we were seated the theatre began its gradual change into darkness.

David appeared, to be hailed by loud and sustained applause, for his reputation was already high in New Orleans. He raised his baton and, glancing over his shoulder up at me, he inclined his head in a short bow and then the baton came down and the music began.

He was perhaps one-third through the overture, when a sour note came from the reed section. It was so raucous that it spoiled the entire mood of the aria. This was quickly followed by the kettle drummer becoming completely confused and finally David's baton was trying to direct a thoroughly disorganized orchestra.

From the audience came irate shouts and hissing. David desperately tried to regain control of the orchestra, but everything had now become confusion. Some of the musicians had stopped playing and were frantically turning music to see where they were. Others kept playing, but were either off key or too nervous to play well.

There was a loud explosion and a puff of smoke on the stage. I saw an object come hurtling from the third level and this also exploded. More and more of these explosions occurred. The hissing and the irate shouting grew louder.

"Torpedoes," Laverne said grimly. "They're throwing torpedoes to show their disapproval."

"What went wrong?" Claude asked in horror. "They were so good at rehearsal. . . ."

I had to shout to be heard above the din. "Are you sure you don't know what went wrong, Mr. Duncan?"

"What?" He bent his head. "Can't hear you. The fools! The blasted idiots! Give the man a chance . . .!" He arose and shouted for attention, but no one paid the slightest heed to him.

Laverne put his lips close to my ear. "I heard what you said. The same thought had come to me."

"Please take me out of here," I begged.

The orchestra was rapidly leaving the pit, escaping more torpedoes which exploded in the midst of them now. The hissing and yelling was louder than ever. As Laverne and I turned to leave the stall, I saw David follow the orchestra and the pit was empty.

Now the audience realized there would be no opera and they grew more enraged than ever. They began tearing at the seats, pulling down draperies, surging toward the stage. Claude still exhorted the audience for quiet and tolerance, but with no more success than before. Laverne and I hastily made our exit before the crowd began leaving. In their present ugly mood some of the violence was bound to carry over to the street.

Laverne hurried me from the area and we finally stopped, breathless, about four blocks away. The French Opera had never seen such a night and likely never would again. Some had wished the performance to begin again, others had clamored for their money back, still others screamed for the scalp of the conductor.

"David's contract and his chances just disappeared," Laverne said sadly. "They'll never let him set foot in the theatre again. We can only hope they don't ride him out of town on a rail. Insulting an opera is high treason in New Orleans."

"Even when all of this trouble was cold-bloodedly arranged?" I said angrily. "Claude did this."

"Well,"—Laverne sounded doubtful, suddenly—"he's an opera lover . . . one of the most profound. It's hard to believe he planned this. . . ."

"Do opera audiences come provided with torpedoes? They must have thrown fifty of them. It was all organized. One man in the orchestra paid to play a sour note, others to follow and upset the entire orchestra until everyone was thrown into such confusion that playing became impossible. This was not by accident, but by design."

"Jana, don't jump to conclusions. . . ."

"How did it happen that I was invited tonight when nobody else was? Or they were warned to stay home? Have you ever seen Celina miss a performance? Or Augusta? Everything had been arranged to destroy David and make me witness his destruction so I'd be properly softened into agreeing to Claude's demands."

"I know. I know it looks evil," Laverne said, "but I still find it hard to convince myself Claude could be responsible."

"Who else then? Not you?"

"No, I swear I was as surprised and shocked as you were. It's a shame, Jana. It's an awful way to have a young musician's career cut off."

"Especially when it wasn't his fault. You know as well as I, that if the rehearsal had not been perfect David would have insisted the performance be postponed. He was ready, so was the orchestra, but someone wrecked everything. David was not to blame for what happened."

"Perhaps Claude will have learned something. . . ."

"Please," I said, "take me home. I don't want to see Claude. I don't want to listen to his lies and his denials. All I wish to do is collect a few things and leave Duncan Plantation. I want to go to David. He's going to need me now."

"Whatever you wish," Laverne said. "We'll pick up the carriage and go back at once."

With the oil lamps on either side of the carriage giving off their yellow light, Laverne and I began our journey in darkness back to the plantation.

"You will return to David now?" Laverne asked after we'd progressed out of the city and were moving along the lonely, dark road back to the mansion.

"Yes, as soon as possible."

"You may not find it easy to leave once Claude gets back to the house. I must warn you about that."

"I will not leave until I tell him what my intentions are. If he tries to stop me, I'll find a way to get out. If he abandons me to the situation I endured when he found me, I'll do my best to fight that too, and with David's help this time. They won't arrest me as a homeless waif."

Laverne was silent for some time. Then he glanced at me. "There's one chance. Just one, and slim at that, but it is there. I feel sure of this."

"Chance for what?" I asked without enthusiasm. I could see no hope for either David or me.

"Any man deserves a second chance. Claude is notorious for not believing in that, but most people in New Orleans do. David was a great success until this happened. I don't think any conductor met with such applause as he. Therefore, some people on the Board of Directors of the opera house are going to think twice."

"No doubt Claude is on the Board," I said.

"He heads it," Laverne said with a sardonic laugh. "His influence is great, his contributions greater. That's not in our favor. If he withdraws his support, the opera house may not survive."

"But the opera is jammed to capacity every performance," I argued.

"True, but it's an expensive operation, my dear. Artists must be brought in from far away. They know how popular opera is in our city, so they raise the fees they demand. We use an augmented orchestra which is highly expensive as well. Therefore, we usually run into a deficit that Claude makes up without a murmur."

"Then David and I are lost," I said. "Until he finds another city and another opportunity."

"There's trouble with that idea too. Claude will never submit a favorable recommendation. Probably David's only chance is to go abroad where Claude's influence won't reach. It's that or the only other alternative."

"What would that be?" I asked. I was too confused to try and think of what Laverne meant.

"Marry Walter, bear his child."

"No."

"Unless you surrender to Claude, David's chances are gone. So you have a clear choice, Jana. One of two things, and you'll have to make up your mind soon. Before David is banished forever."

"I have to talk to David," I said.

"Of course. See him tomorrow. If he thinks he has a chance to go elsewhere and this frightful thing tonight won't keep him from finding a good place to conduct, then go away with him, by all means."

"David's success means so much to him," I said. "He's devoted his life to it and he's good. He could become one of the most famous orchestra leaders in the world. Shall I take away all his chances to accomplish that?"

"If you are asking me for a direct and honest answer," Laverne said, "I think you should marry him, go away and let him try again. With you beside him, with his talent, he should make it. He may need time and there may be privation for both of you, but I have confidence David will overcome what happened tonight."

"I wish I were as sure," I said.

"Jana, you and David are perfectly suited to one another. Now I'm not a rich man, but if you decide to go away with him, I will give you as a wedding present sufficient money so that you will not be in actual want while David builds his reputation again."

"You are a dear," I said, and his offer did restore my spirts somewhat. "I'm sure David would never accept your offer, but I do appreciate it."

"I am distressed to see two fine young people with such brilliant futures, robbed of everything because of the personal grasp for glory of one man. Claude wants a grandchild so the line will not die, so the dynasty will continue. Perhaps he thinks he will live again in the person of this grandchild. I don't know, but it wouldn't surprise me. That is why I made the offer and why it will stand indefinitely."

"I'll talk to Claude tonight, if he comes home," I said. "Tomorrow I'll see David. Until then, I have no answers and I find that I cannot make up my mind. Be patient with me, Mr. Cavet."

"If you refuse his offer," Laverne persisted, "he will do his utmost to return you to a state of poverty so that you will be taken into custody again. It will all be arranged. Claude will take any steps to force you to agree. I know him. This is my warning. You will not find it easy to defy him, but I urge you to do so."

"I'll know what to do by this time tomorrow," I said. "Whatever I decide I shall always be grateful to you."

We didn't talk much after that. I was sick with worry, tired, despairing of finding an answer, longing to see David and comfort him if I could. I knew the disappointment he must be going through.

When we turned onto the Duncan estate the great mansion lay before us in darkness, except for a single weak light left just inside the front door.

"I'll drive the carriage around to the stable and wake up the hostler," Laverne said. "Do you wish me at your side when you speak to Claude?"

"No, thank you. But I prefer to be alone at that time, if you don't mind."

"I really don't," he said with a humorless smile. "Quite likely it's better that I not be there, because I'm sure to lose my temper and tell Claude precisely what I think of him. There's little sense in making him angrier than he is now. But I won't be far off if you need me."

134

"I only wish to hear what he has to say. There will be no trouble. Thank you again."

He dropped me off and I made my way into the darkened house, pausing to light some of the lamps. I carried one up the staircase to my rooms. There I tried to compose myself for what might turn into a stormy talk with Claude. I seated myself near a window overlooking the approaches to the mansion and I tried, vainly as it turned out, to find some way to avoid Claude's certain demand that I marry Walter and yet, in some manner, save David from the oblivion that could envelop him as a failure.

I heard Laverne return and go to his rooms. For an hour I sat near the window. When Claude's buggy turned off the main road, I picked up a lamp and lighted my way downstairs. I waited until he returned from the stables and I opened the door for him.

"I didn't expect to find you up, my dear Jana," he said.

"I must talk to you tonight. Now! Please, Mr. Duncan. It's very important to me."

He took my elbow and guided me across the drawing room to the library. "It's important to me as well. I'm sure we can find a solution to the problem."

He set my lamp on the desk, lit the large one also on the desk and a third which stood on a table behind me. He made sure the door was closed tightly before he sat down.

"I shall speak first," he said. "I know you will accuse me of arranging that fiasco tonight at the opera house. Whether I did or not has no bearing on the question we must solve. I can tell you now that David is in a great deal of trouble. Oh, he has defenders. Anyone in trouble usually does. But there are more against him than for him. Opera in New Orleans is vitally important. We can take no chances on giving contracts to people with mediocre talents."

"David is far from being mediocre and you know it," I said angrily.

"Let's say I concede that. David will not get his contract, of course. Tomorrow he will be invited to leave New Orleans and he will not take with him any letters attesting to his ability. Rather, the news of what happened will be published in many newspapers, probably all over the world. I would say, bluntly, that David's career is over."

"Then why must we go through all this?" I asked.

"Because, my dear girl, I can reinstate him if I choose. The Board will listen to me. They will give David one more chance and if you are that sure of his ability, you know very well that he'll make it and once again be in line to take over the music at the French Opera House."

"You are sure you can do this?" I asked.

"I know I can. Jana, my dear Jana, I admit I had something to do with what happened. It was the only way I could make you listen to me. I had to do that and I would again."

"In other words, if I agree to marry Walter, David will have his chance and he will make good at it. If I refuse, David's career will be lost."

Claude bowed his head slightly. "I'm afraid you are about correct. Now, before you condemn me for what I have done, hear me out. Try to find some compassion in your heart for me. I need a grandson. I must have one. If Walter alone bears my name after I die, everything I've worked for will vanish. When Walter dies, so will the name. I must protect it, perpetuate it, because it represents so much. I will leave my grandson a fortune in money and more power than he will ever need. I'll leave him a plantation that will keep growing, a fortune he can do a great deal of good with. I am not a selfish man, and I don't expect my grandson will be. I shall drill this into him, that money means he will lack for nothing and he will find it gives him influence, but also it must be shared. Some of the fortune must be turned into things everyone can enjoy."

I stifled an almost uncontrollable urge to walk out on him without another word, to commandeer a buggy, drive to New Orleans and leave with David at once. "Walter does not wish to marry me," I said.

"Walter has no idea what's good for him. He'll marry you."

"Suppose he does not?" I asked.

"My dear, I tell you he'll do whatever I say."

"And supposing Marie turns up?"

"She will not. She's been gone too long. More than a year. No . . . no, it will be a year in just a day or two. She won't be back. I think she had a secret lover and ran off with him. I have already taken steps to have her declared legally dead. That should be accomplished soon. Immediately afterwards you will marry Walter."

"By that time David's reputation will be ruined beyond any hope of repair," I said.

"Quite true. But if you give me your word . . . and I'll accept it . . . that you will marry Walter, I shall see that David is given another chance. You know I can do this."

"Why me?" I asked in my depths of despair. "Why not some other girl who isn't in love with someone else?"

"My grandchild must have good blood in him. Exceptional blood lines are not easy to find. With your ancestors, your upbringing, I know what I'm getting. There can be no one else. I made up my mind to that long ago."

"I wish to talk to David before I make up my mind," I said.

"Of course. Anything you wish. Be sure to inform the young man that he will lead the orchestra when we will again put on the new opera. Tell him he will find a receptive and sympathetic audience and that his career as a great musical director will have begun."

"There is still one other problem," I said. "Don't make light of it, Mr. Duncan, because it's real. My life is in danger so long as I'm here. I don't know why nor who is behind it, but I've been close to being killed twice."

"I promise you I'll take every measure to see that you are protected and happy."

"Should Marie return before I marry Walter, you must promise me this arrangement is off. I am then free to marry David and you will not take any steps to destroy him."

"Very well. Marie isn't coming back, not after all this time. I agree."

"I shall talk to you again tomorrow evening," I said. "Tomorrow I'll drive to New Orleans and speak of all this to David."

Claude shook his head. "My dear, it will be your decision, not David's. He will implore you not to give in to me, but I'm sure you see the sense to it. The more you think about this, the more you know I'm right. Bear Walter's son and there is little on this earth you may not have. Nothing that I will not do for you."

I arose. "Good night, Mr. Duncan," I said.

I fled from the room and upstairs to my own suite before I broke down and wept. I didn't want him to see that. Neither Claude nor anyone else.

I already knew what I was going to tell David. My mind had been made up after my talk with Laverne Cavet. Claude's offer only strengthened my resolve. I must make David see it my way—for his sake.

Thirteen

I slept, though it was far from restful. Twice I almost got up to dress and go to New Orleans, even though it was hours until daylight. As it was, I left the plantation at first light, without seeing anybody with the exception of the sleepy-eyed, irritable hostler.

New Orleans was still in the process of waking up when I arrived, though the streets were already quite busy and the almost usual din and confusion were evident.

I turned the buggy over to a stable, walked the rather considerable distance to David's hotel, which was not situated in a section where most of the more ornate buildings were located.

The desk clerk sent a boy to awaken David and tell him I was in the restaurant. David came down in five minutes. He hadn't slept well either and had been up since dawn.

With a total disregard for propriety, I went into his arms and kissed him fondly before we sat down at the table where a smiling waitress took our order.

"I spoke to Claude last night," I said.

"I suppose he denied having had anything to do with the plan to stop my career?"

"No, David. He admitted it."

"He'd have had to. How could he deny it anyway? An audience coming to the opera with pockets full of torpedoes. It had to be planned and, of course, I soon discovered it was. Two of my musicians admitted they'd been paid to play badly and throw the whole orchestra off. I tried to get their confessions printed in the newspaper so everyone can learn the truth of what happened, but . . . you can guess how that turned out."

"Claude either owns the newspapers or dominates them," I said. "I know, darling."

"What did he tell you besides admitting he wrecked my career?"

"If I agree to marry Walter, he will ask the Board running the French Opera House to give you another chance."

"I don't want it," he said bitterly. "I'm finished with this city . . . I . . . what am I saying?" He bent his head for a moment. "Of course I want another chance, but not under those terms."

"Laverne Cavet has offered to help us," I said.

"So we have one friend at least. What good will his help be? He is in no position to influence the Board."

"What will we do?" I asked.

"Truthfully, before I was told you were waiting, I'd been busy packing. I have enough money to get both of us out of town. I'll find work somewhere, any kind of work, and begin building for another opportunity to put together an orchestra. It won't be easy. . . ."

"Darling," I said, my heart aching for him, "it's not possible. Claude will intervene every time you try to return to your profession. He has connections everywhere. It's hopeless."

David looked up quickly. "You're not going to marry that lout?"

"I want you to have your chance at success," I said.

"I will not permit it. Besides, there's another reason you can't stay here. Or have you forgotten that someone has been trying to kill you?"

"I haven't forgotten."

"Another thing. I'm not sure whether Marie is dead or alive. I spent some time learning all I could about her. She married Walter because of his father's money. She used to make fun of Walter, sometimes in front of him. She openly admitted that she hated Claude and

140

everybody else at the plantation. She made Walter jump through hoops. And he took it."

"He was in love with her. He still is," I said.

"And yet his father insists he marry you?"

"Yes, and Walter will agree to it."

"You will not," he said with finality.

My heart ached for him. Everything he ever wanted to be he was about to sacrifice for my sake. He would insist upon it. If I told him I also intended to surrender to Claude, he'd have none of it and he'd not only wreck his chances even more, but there might be violence as well.

"There may be yet a chance that Claude may change his mind," I said. "Before I make up mine, I want another talk with him. There's no hurry, darling. He still has to get that court order declaring Marie dead."

"What's the difference? If I don't direct the orchestra next performance, I'll have lost my chances. Another thing, I'm not so sure we have that much time."

"But there's a week . . . at least. . . ."

"Jana, it may be that Claude won't need a court order declaring Marie dead. She may, in fact, really be dead now."

I was aghast. "What makes you think so?"

"I talked to some of her people—her family. They all insist that Marie would not have gone off on her own accord. She was devoted to all of them and with her marriage to Walter she could provide for them very well. She did so, as long as she was at the plantation. They said she would have told them she was running away. Or, at the very least, have written them when she was safe from the Duncan family. Every last relative Marie has, swears she must be dead."

"But how? Why hasn't her body been discovered?"

"A body can be hidden in a thousand places. The river washes them into the gulf, or they snag below the surface of the river and stay there. Or they can be buried . . . getting rid of a body is easy here."

141

"Do you think she was murdered?"

"Not necessarily, though the thought did come to me. She could have met with an accident. She's been gone a year . . . or close to it."

"A year just short of a few more days. Claude told me."

David was silent a moment. "Claude seems to have kept track of the date rather well."

"Because he needs it to get the court order he's after," I reminded him.

David nodded. "Of course. I'm just naturally suspicious of everyone, I guess. And I admit I'm confused and I'm scared."

"I wonder if Walter could have killed her," I said thoughtfully. "He's a strange man. In fact, as Laverne pointed out, he's almost two different men. He may be giving the illusion that he's still madly in love with Marie to avoid arousing any suspicion against him."

"It's possible," David admitted. "There's one thing we can't overlook. You came here knowing no one. Not even Claude. So you could hardly have brought with you a motive for your murder. The motive had to come to life after you arrived. Therefore it must be tied to the Duncan family. Your death is important to someone right here in this city, or on the plantation. Therefore, it has to be connected with Marie's disappearance or, Claude's insistence you marry Walter."

"I see no motive," I said. "My death wouldn't bring Marie back, nor even establish the fact that she's dead. How could my death benefit anyone at the plantation when they all want the Duncan dynasty to go on, and I can provide the means to accomplish that ambition on their part. In fact, my death would ruin all their plans."

"I don't know," David said dispiritedly. "We've so little to go on."

"Is it possible that Marie might have been in love with someone else and gone off with him?" I asked.

"Marie's father said she was acting better just before she disappeared. By that I mean she'd been a disappoint-

142

ment to the Duncans and they were making things unpleasant. For weeks she'd been morose and temperamental, but she changed, according to her father. He is of the opinion she met someone else."

"But no proof of anything," I said. All this while my mind was seeking some way to make David postpone his plan to take me away. He must have his chance, no matter what happened to me. I loved him far too well to allow his life to be wrecked because of me. In my desperation for a reason to delay things, I happened on one idea. A fantastic one so far as I was concerned, but it might work.

"As you say, we have a little time. David, I wish a favor of you. It's something I've thought about often. Will you go back up the river to the place where the packet blew up and sank? Just to make certain no trace has ever been found of Papa and Mama?"

"Jana, it . . . it's not possible. You saw what happened when the gun powder barrels blew and the boilers exploded. All of this happened close to your cabin. There isn't a solitary chance. . . ."

"I have to be sure. I never did anything about searching for them. At least I might give them a decent burial. I can't help it. I know the whole thing sounds silly, but that's the way it is with me. If you can't go there, I'll have to. Because I must be completely satisfied that there is nothing to be done before I leave this region."

"I'll go," he said. "There's a packet or two leaving every night. I'll be there in the morning and see what I can discover."

"Please don't think this just a foolish whim. I loved them so. I can't be content until I know."

"It will give me something to do."

"Thank you, David. I'll be able to leave here with a lighter heart once I feel I've at least tried to do something."

"Consider it done."

143

"What of the musicians?" I asked. "How do you feel about what happened?"

David seemed to relax, as if some of the tension went away because my question could be answered with a degree of pleasure.

"They are musicians," he said. "They know exactly what happened. They know I had nothing to do with it. The men who deliberately threw us off have been discharged. The others want me to take over. They've said so publicly and they have drawn up a petition to place before the Board. They also told me that if I agreed, they'd refuse to play at that theatre again unless I was given another chance."

"How nice of them," I said. "Such a petition could go a long way. I'm not so sure about the threat to quit."

"I'm afraid it wouldn't work. Claude Duncan would let the theatre fall into ruins if it would help him get a grandchild. He's obsessed with that determination. Just when he was about to look for a girl to take Marie's place, you came along. I can't say I blame him for choosing you."

We had completed our breakfast, but we dawdled over more coffee until we realized people were waiting for our table.

"I'll meet you here day after tomorrow," I said. "Meantime, I'll do all I can to change Claude's mind."

"I'll talk to him when I get back. That is, if I can get near him. I wish I could insist you stay in town all day. I've seen so little of you, but I'm rehearsing the orchestra today. Nobody has tried to stop us. We want to be ready if we get another opportunity to play."

"You should have told me," I said. "I'd have taken less of your time."

"We don't begin practice at nine o'clock in the morning," he said with a smile. "We're early today."

He walked me to the stable where I reclaimed my horse and buggy. I drove him to the opera house where the

144

rehearsals were to be held. David stood beside the buggy for a moment after I pulled up.

"I wish I knew what you're up to," he said. "I have a feeling there's some scheme hatching in your mind. Please, Jana, don't give in to Claude. Remember that there's only one thing I want. It towers above ambition by a mile. I want you."

"We'll be together soon," I said.

"Take care. Don't forget those attempts on your life."

"I'll be watchful," I promised. "Don't worry about me. Do what you can to find if anyone was taken from the river who resembled Papa or Mama."

"Day after tomorrow," he said. "At the restaurant in my hotel. For breakfast."

"I'll be there," I said.

"Please be careful, Jana. I don't want you to go back to the plantation. You could be in great danger and I won't be near you to help."

"I hope I can arrange something so you get your second chance. That's worth any risk. But I will be careful. And thank you for trying to learn what you can about my mother and father. I feel if there is anything, I have to know."

He stood, hat in hand, watching me drive away. I waved as I reached a corner and turned down another street. Then all the hopelessness returned, for I had lied to David. I was going back to the plantation to tell Claude that I would marry Walter if he gave David a chance and sponsored him before the Board.

I knew how well Claude could destroy David's musical career forever. Without it David would be lost, and so would I. If we defied Claude, we'd never find the happiness which David deserved. It was better that I obey Claude's edict and let David move on to his certain success. I'd find some happiness in knowing he would reach the highest point in his field.

The horse jogged along. I didn't require any speed on this trip back to the plantation. Only the fact that what I was about to do would insure David's future, kept me from breaking down. I tried to convince myself there were worse things than marrying the son of the richest and most powerful man in New Orleans, but it didn't work. Wealth and power to me were only a means to an end of putting David straight on the path he'd sought so long.

I made up my mind that I'd be as good a wife to Walter as possible. Since he was no more in love with me than I was with him, there should be few problems in our marriage. He'd never forget Marie and I'd never forget David.

Laverne had been staying at the plantation and when I arrived he was just returning from a late morning ride. He saw me and rode alongside the buggy until we reached the stables. There he dismounted and helped me down while the hostler took charge of the animals.

"You saw David?" Laverne asked me as we strolled back to the house.

"Yes. He knows that Claude manipulated that whole horrible affair and that he actually paid some of the members of the orchestra to throw the overture off so that it would look like the results of David's bad conducting."

"I believe I once mentioned that Claude was a ruthless man. If I didn't, you know it now. What will you do?"

"Marry Walter. It will break my heart, but that's the only way David will have his chance."

"Did he agree to that?" Laverne asked indignantly.

"David thinks I'll join him in a few days and we'll leave New Orleans. He's gone off on business and when he gets back I hope I can find the courage to tell him."

"You'll inform Claude that you agree to his terms?"

"Yes, at once. Because when David returns, I want everything ready so he can conduct at the next performance."

"It's more than I think I'd do," Laverne said sadly. "I wouldn't have the courage to sacrifice my life for someone else. Perhaps I can talk Claude into not insisting on this madness."

"No one can, but thank you," I said. "You're the only person who sympathizes with me. At least openly."

"I'm not a Duncan," he said. "I can stand up to Claude and not suffer any consequences more grave than being banished from this house. Which is a matter I may arrange myself. I'm afraid I won't be able to abide Claude after this."

"I know Celina and Augusta both fear him. I think Augusta would like to help, but there is nothing she can do."

"Don't count on Augusta too much," he warned. "I've seen her do more than one about face, and not for the better. She depends on Claude for everything and she's not apt to cross him, nor even condemn him."

Coleen must have seen us approaching, for she had the door open as we crossed the porch.

"I'm to tell you," she said, "that the master is waiting in the library, mum."

So Claude must have seen us approaching and he didn't intend to lose any time.

"Does that include me?" Laverne asked.

"He didn't say your name, sir."

"Well, he's going to enjoy my company anyway. Come along, Jana, and we'll face the dragon together."

Claude was seated behind his desk. He seemed surprised that Laverne accompanied me and not very pleased, but Laverne closed the door and sat down without invitation.

"I hope you had a productive visit with your David," Claude said.

"I talked to him, Mr. Duncan. He wants me to leave New Orleans with him."

"That is a decision you must make," Claude said. "You realize David will have no future in the only line of work he is skilled at."

"If it were me," Laverne commented, "I'd as soon dig ditches."

"No one asked your opinion," Claude said tartly. "What will you do, Jana?"

"You swear to me that David will have his chance?"

"You have my solemn word and I never go back on it. Laverne can attest to that."

"It's true," Laverne said. "That's the only favorable thing I'll say about this dirty business. You ought to be ashamed of yourself, Claude."

Claude disregarded that.

"The same opera is to be premièred again," I said. "David will conduct?"

"I have your word. That's enough for me, Jana. David will conduct. The following day, after you marry Walter, David will be granted a substantial contract and I shall see to it that his name and his talent are heard of around the world. Within a year he'll be famous, for the young man is exceptionally talented and it will be my pleasure to sponsor him."

"What a two-faced way of doing things," Laverne commented. "The girl gives up everything, marries a man she does not love, has children, not to add to the happiness of herself or her husband, but for the sake of preserving the Duncan name because their grandfather insists upon it. If I didn't know you the way I do, I'd say you were mad."

"You are excused," Claude said quietly.

"Not quite yet. You made this young lady an offer. Put it in writing, my friend. Your word has always been good with me, but in this particular case I've decided not to trust you. Jana, insist he give you an air-tight contract."

"There is no need for that," I said.

"It's a business deal. Handle it like business and, if you like, I'll have my lawyer go over it."

"I said you are no longer needed!" Claude's voice was sharper.

Laverne was on his feet. "If you are ordering me out

148

of this room, you are ordering me out of this house and your life, Claude."

"I'm asking you to leave, Laverne. I don't care how you take it, nor what you do."

Laverne turned to me. "I offered to help. I have enough to guarantee the running of the French Opera, the same sum Claude provides each year. David doesn't need Claude's help."

For a moment my heart soared. "Do you——?" I began, but Claude's voice overrode mine.

"Listen to me," he warned. "If you cross me, I'll break you. Perpetuating my name is far more important to me than your friendship, valued as it may be. Do not interfere, Laverne."

I knew the threat wasn't idle. Not trusting my voice, I shook my head at Laverne.

"The offer still holds," Laverne told me. "Come see me any time. I can handle this and I'd like to. For once I'd enjoy seeing Claude not have his own way."

"Get out of here." Claude half arose as if to add force to his order.

Laverne looked unimpressed. "I can tell you this now," he said to me, "without risking my friendship with that monster behind the desk. There is no friendship any longer. There never should have been from the moment I knew he hired two men to attack David and beat him to a point where he'd gladly withdraw from any connection with New Orleans, the French Opera House, or the Duncan family. It's a wonder to me he didn't order the men to kill David."

"It that true?" I asked Claude.

"Yes. I thought that the better way to break up anything between the two of you."

"Now you know what manner of man he is," Laverne said. "I've known it all along, and that makes me almost as bad as he. I'm clearing out."

He pulled the door open savagely, slammed it behind

him. I saw the dismay on Claude's face. The breaking of this friendship did affect him.

"At least that mystery is solved," I said. I spoke calmly because if I let my emotions slip out of the tight grasp I had on them, I'd be lost. "Is it also possible that you arranged to have a dead branch placed at the stone wall jump so that I'd be thrown? Is it possible that you, or someone you paid, followed me to the bank of the river, threw me into the water and attempted to stone me to death?"

"I swear I had nothing to do with that," Claude said earnestly.

"The mind that concocted a mad scheme to get rid of David by nearly killing him could have thought up those other attempts and not hesitated to put them into practice."

"Why would I want you harmed? I told you before. I want the healthiest possible mother for my grandson. A woman sound of mind and body. I would be defeating my own purposes by harming you."

I inclined my head slightly. "I have to agree, Mr. Duncan. Of anyone I might suspect, you have the least reason to wish me harm, the best reason to insure my safety. I brought it up because Laverne revealed the truth about the attack on David."

"Laverne ought to know better." He studied my face for a moment. "Jana, you can be perfectly frank with me. Is Laverne really in love with you?"

"Perhaps he is. I'm not sure."

"I don't know about him. He's been acting strangely of late. I've never known him to be so nervous, but he's probably taking this too much at heart. He certainly demonstrated that just now. Well, my dear, I'm glad you changed your attitude and that you will become a member of my family. It makes me very proud and happy."

"I wish it did the same for me," I said. "As Laverne put it, this is a business transaction, not a romance."

"Ah, then you wish a written contract?"

"Of course I don't. At any rate, it isn't necessary because I won't marry Walter until after David's success is assured."

"Then perhaps it is I who should insist on a contract."

"If you wish it," I said.

He arose, walked around the desk and took my hands to lift me from the chair. "Jana, my dear, I have never liked anyone quite as much as I do you. If you become the mother of my grandchildren, they are bound to be as you are. Not as my son is. He shows a weakness in the blood line. You will strengthen it again. I have the utmost admiration for you. There is nothing you couldn't wish for that I would not grant you."

"The one thing you could grant me you will not," I said. "Anything else is of no importance. May I go now?"

"Of course. Don't be angry. Consider my position too."

"Good morning," I said tersely and I left him. Before I was halfway along the drawing room, he stepped out of the library and called after me.

"Marie will be declared legally dead in one week. You will marry Walter one hour after the court makes the declaration. The kind of wedding you may wish is up to you."

The kind of wedding I wanted wouldn't occur now. I brought my hands to my eyes to hide the tears and I fled upstairs to my rooms.

It was done. Agreed upon. David would be heart-broken when I told him. Yet, this had to be. There were times when the heart must not be permitted to think for the brain and this was one of them.

I threw myself across the bed and gave way entirely to the tears that would no longer be checked.

Fourteen

I got through the day, somehow. At the supper table Walter was glum and uncommunicative. Celina was as serene as ever, Augusta gave me several little smiles of sympathy and Claude was at his mellow best, relating experiences in the fields and some anecdotes from his younger days. He was especially solicitous of me.

After supper I went directly to my rooms, pretending a headache which soon wasn't pretense. Celina tapped on the door and came in with a sleeping draught in its pink paper.

"I thought you might need this, Jana. Claude has told me about his plans for you and Walter. I will not insult you with wishes for your happiness. I know what you are giving up and I admire you for it. Claude will never change. Whatever he wants he goes after and he's never known defeat. I sometimes wish he would."

"I'm going to try to make the best of it," I said. "You do realize that Walter isn't in love with me."

"He's never stopped being in love with that awful woman who walked out on him."

"Poor Walter. I once hated him for his dangerous tricks, but now I know why he did these things. I can't hate him any longer."

"Walter needs a great deal of understanding," Celina confessed. "I admit I don't know how to handle him sometimes. Ordinarily he's gentle. Not precisely honest, I must say, but not looking for a chance to hurt anyone. And then, if he is sufficiently aroused, I sometimes think he is capable of killing all of us."

"One day," I said, "the mystery of Marie's disappearance will be solved. Perhaps then he'll settle down."

"It's more likely you will settle him down as his wife. He needs a strong hand and something tells me you have it. At least he'll respect you. Now I know you're tired, so I'll say good night."

"Thank you for the sleeping draught," I said. "I do need some sound rest."

She kissed me on the cheek and suddenly I knew her to be a warm, tender woman hiding her true feelings under a stern mask because that was the way Claude would have her be.

I prepared the sleeping draught, blew out the last lamp, lay back in bed and thought about this day which was to govern my whole lifetime. I told myself a dozen times my decision was right. David's talent must not be allowed to go to waste. This was the only way I could help him and I prayed that he'd understand. Telling him my decision was going to be the most awful moment of my life.

I took the sleeping draught in self-defense against my doubts which had a way of building during the night hours. I fell into a deep sleep soon afterwards.

My last thoughts, slightly confused by the growing effects of the draught, were concerned with my complete vulnerability while I was under the influence of the drug.

This must have impressed itself on my mind so firmly that when I awakened in full daylight, I actually felt surprised that I had. I also felt rested and my headache had vanished. I stood before the window to see that it was a bright, cheerful day. I looked out over the vastness of the estate and the plantation and shook my head to think that I would have a share in all this wealth.

I went down to breakfast which I ate alone. Odette served me without a smile or a word. Her dark eyes studied my face with the same expression she'd use in observing a speck of dust—something to be rid of.

I had to keep up my spirits somehow, so I risked going out for a walk. Against my better judgment and

David's suggestions, but I wanted to feel the sun and breathe in the fresh, flower-scented air.

As I made my slow way along the paths between the flower gardens, I was surprised to see Augusta picking up her skirt to follow me. I waited for her.

"Good morning," I said. "I should have asked you if you wished to take the air with me."

"Oh no. I rarely do that, it seems. I wanted to talk to you—when there was no chance of anyone listening. I'm afraid of them. I really am."

"Them? Do you mean your sister and Claude?"

"They could force me to leave the plantation and I don't know where I'd go. That makes me afraid of them. I don't want them to have any reason to act against me."

"Now, Augusta, whatever reason could they find? You are incapable of hurting anyone."

"Oh, I don't know about that. There are times when my thoughts are not gentle. I even . . . thought angry thoughts about you."

"I don't believe it," I said.

"Oh, but it's true! You came here—an interloper, I must say. Until you arrived, I felt that one day Celina and I would share in the handling of this estate. I'm sure Claude would not have granted control of it to poor Walter, who has demonstrated how incapable he is on many occasions. So you see, I felt that you were cheating me out of my share of the estate. But I don't feel that way any longer."

"Augusta, if by some chance I should have a say in the operation of this property, I swear that I would never even think of not including you in everything that was done here. Of all things, to worry about being forced to leave."

"I only told you because I wanted you to know I'm not the self-effacing, timid old maid that I seem to be. I can get angry too. As I am now, for I hate what Claude has done."

155

"It's Claude's way," I said. "I'll manage to reconcile myself to it."

"Will you have a big wedding?" she asked in all innocence. "Marie insisted on a most lavish one."

"I doubt it. I'm sure Walter would prefer it to be quiet and private."

"Yes, I suppose so. Seems a shame though, to spoil such an occasion. My sister told me she'd talked to you last night. A most satisfactory talk, she said. You know she and I can handle Claude. Oh yes. We can handle him easily, so come to us if you wish help in some matter which he opposes. Provided it isn't very important. If we didn't like you, we should never have made such an offer, but it holds true."

"Thank you, Augusta." This gentle creature, telling me she was capable of evil and dire thoughts. It would have been highly amusing if I didn't think so well of her.

"Let's forget all our troubles for a little while," she suggested, "and enjoy the flowers and the sun. I do love it here. My heart would be broken if I had to leave. No, more than that. I think I'd die. Yes, I actually think so."

I enjoyed her company. It helped to lighten this otherwise worrisome day. At dinner everything went well, possibly because Claude was not present. Afterwards, I went to my rooms to see if I could rest a bit and try to formulate in my mind the way in which I would tell David what my decision was. I hoped he would understand.

It was late afternoon when Coleen tapped on my door and came in with a letter in her hand. "This came for you, mum. I brought it right up."

I saw that it was an ordinary envelope, properly stamped and mailed from the town upstate where the packet had blown up and Papa and Mama had died. At first I thought it was from David, but the writing seemed to be in a woman's hand.

"I come with an offer to help you, mum," Coleen

broke in on my thoughts. "It's come to my mind that you and Walter are to be married, much as you do not wish this marriage. So, if you like, I will discuss it with several of my brothers and many of my cousins and I shall fix it that the boys from the Irish Channel will have a little talk, as it were, with the bridegroom and sort of discourage him a bit."

"Please don't do that," I implored her. "I know you mean well, but I wish no trouble, and really Walter is not to blame for any of this."

"I'll do as you say, mum. But don't let that Walter fool you. He's a bad 'un when he wants to be."

"I'm afraid we all are, Coleen. Were you in this household when Marie vanished?"

"Yes'm. I think I know what happened to her."

"To Marie? You know why she vanished?"

"Yes'm. I know why, but I ain't so sure how. Marie was not faithful to Walter. And she didn't care if he knew it. She used to make fun of him all the time. He'd get mad at her, but he wouldn't touch her because he said he loved her too much. But a man can't take that sort of treatment forever."

"What do you mean by that?" I asked.

"She was seeing somebody regular, she was. Slipping away and returning like a thief."

"Whom did she see?"

"I don't know that. Nobody does, I guess, except the man himself."

"And Marie." I was leading her on gently so she wouldn't become confused.

"Not Marie. I think she's dead."

"Coleen, you must be sure to make such a statement."

"I'm knowing that, but there's Walter. He has a bad temper, that one. He loved her. If she was going off with someone, he could have killed her. Now ain't that an answer to her disappearance? Maybe, that is. I don't know for sure, but that's how we're all thinking."

"Coleen, I appreciate your wishing to help, but please

don't make such statements to anyone else. You cannot be certain that what you say is true and it's a terrible accusation to make."

"I've told none but you, mum, and I won't say it again."

"Thank you. I do appreciate your fine intentions."

She bobbed a quick curtsy and left me. I examined the envelope again. It was addressed to me here at the plantation, but I knew no one in that upriver town. Holding that envelope, I had the strangest sense of foreboding.

I tore the flap open and read the brief note inside while my consternation grew with each word.

Miss Jana Stewart:

I write this so you will not marry Walter Duncan. He cannot marry, for he has a wife already. One who knows all the dark secrets of the Duncan family and who wishes to impart them to you before it is too late. If I come to the plantation, Claude Duncan will have me done away with, so you must come to me. Secretly, for I put nothing past that terrible man. Tonight at ten o'clock, fetch a horse from the stable and ride down to the river. There you will turn North and ride until you come to the steamship graveyard where there are several packets rotting away. You will see the *Prince Maximilian* plain enough, for the name is on the bow. I will be waiting for you aboard her. If I am late, wait for me. I will not fail you and you must not fail me. Be sure to come alone, else you will not find me.

Marie Duncan

I slowly let the letter flutter to my lap and I sat in utter amazement. Marie had returned! Quite likely she'd heard of the impending marriage and decided it was

158

time to reassert her position in this household. It was a way out for me. Not even Claude could hold me to my promise if Marie was back. He couldn't then obtain a court order saying she was dead, and she was bound to fight any divorce proceedings he might contemplate for his son.

My hopes bounded to the sky. I would have a difficult time waiting until the hour when I'd start out to meet her. Of course I couldn't confide in anyone. Possibly I might have showed the letter to Laverne, but he had left the plantation and I doubted he'd ever come back.

I had to restrain myself at supper, for the joy building within me threatened to spill over and if it did, Claude would instantly realize something had happened. Of all people he must not know that Marie was alive and back. He would take immediate steps to handle such a situation and it might not be to my benefit. Certainly not to Marie's. Walter was his usual somber self. I was really tempted to tell him, for he deserved to know, but he'd have never been able to keep it secret.

I wondered what Marie wanted, what she intended to do. I hoped that if she offered to withdraw and give Walter a divorce, I could convince her not to make that offer to Claude. At least not for some time. I knew I could make her understand that I had no designs on her husband or her marriage. I didn't care how she handled Claude. I would even wish her luck in getting whatever she wanted out of him.

She must have only gone this short distance—fifty miles or so—upriver. Had she run off with someone, I was sure she'd have gone further than that, for she would have known that Claude would hunt her down if he could. I knew, of course, that Claude never had any such intentions, for he was well rid of her, but she'd hardly see it in that light.

I thought the time would never come and when it did, Claude and Celina were downstairs in the drawing room, so that I had to slip down the back stairs and leave by way of the rear door.

I hurried to the stable. This time I didn't even want the hostler to know I'd ridden off, so I crept into the tack room, selected a blanket and saddle, carried them outside and all the way down to the biggest barn. I left them there while I returned for a horse.

Moving slowly so the animal wouldn't make much noise, I led her down to the barn. There I saddled her and walked her a good distance away before I mounted and flicked at her with my crop.

Riding through this darkness was not my idea of a safe journey, and it occurred to me that I was violating all of the edicts handed down by David, Laverne and the others. It was not safe for me to venture far alone. Yet here I was riding through the darkness, trusting to the horse not to make any misstep. And finally it occurred to me that this might might be a trap. It was possible that the letter was a hoax, a sure way of getting me out of the house and far enough away that I could be disposed of easily without arousing anyone.

I felt cold chills run up and down my spine. I was being foolish and contrary to do such a thing as this. No matter if Marie wished secrecy, I should have told someone. Yet I kept on my way, conscious of the risk and equally aware that I must accept it.

It was a long ride, but not too difficult, once I was on the road. It skirted the river, was used heavily by day, so that it was worn smooth. Once I heard a farm wagon filled with roistering riverboat hands trundling in my direction, so I promptly left the road, took refuge among the cypresses beside the river and let them go by.

I had time to think now. Mostly about the letter and about Marie. With her help I might be able to find my way out of this maze. Once Claude knew his hands were tied, he'd have no further cause to destroy David's career and he'd not stand in the way of our marriage. If I guessed properly, Marie was not going to give in to

Claude easily, perhaps never. Her ability to stand up against him would be made all but trouble-proof if Walter asserted his enduring love for her. Not even a court predisposed toward Claude would dare hand down a verdict in a situation of that kind. More and more my hopes began to rise.

Marie's return might even remove the danger which had threatened me since I arrived. I'd given studious consideration to every suspect I could think of and I'd ended up by recognizing only one as a man with a motive that made my death necessary.

Claude had no reason, nor did Celina, his wife. They wanted me alive. Augusta seemed incapable of anything to do with violence. Laverne was on my side, strenuously trying to help me, even to the point of defying Claude and losing his long-standing friendship. That left Walter.

Walter did not wish to marry me or anyone else. He was waiting for Marie to return. If his father insisted he marry me, then Walter might have seen one solution. Get rid of me. If he couldn't scare me away, he could kill me. He could easily have arranged that dead branch at the jump. He was husky enough to have thrown me into the river and then hurled heavy rocks at me. He was a strange young man, one of moods and temperament. I stood in the way of his ever bringing Marie back; therefore, I must be removed. That was his motive, the only one I could think of, and it pointed straight at Walter.

I hoped with all my heart that Marie would be waiting for me and I could convince her to return to her husband. I'd not only make him supremely happy, but I'd put an end to the mischief Claude was creating by his mad determination to hold a grandson in his arms before he died.

There was some kind of a tavern or inn at a cross road which I also avoided by making a wide circle around it. I tried to read the dial of my lapel watch, but it was too dark to see the hands. I judged I had at least another half hour to the rendezvous time. I was not far

161

away now. I'd heard talk about the steamship graveyard and while I'd never seen it, I knew just about where it was located.

This was where old steamboats which had outlived their usefulness were brought. So were the wrecks of those holed open by snags, those with their sterns blown off by the explosion of the boilers. Others which had burned and were beyond rebuilding. I expected to find four or five of them rotting away in this backwash of the river, but when I arrived, I saw the dark shrouded outlines of a score of these useless relics left there to fall apart, which many of them were doing.

There were no lights, but the decks, the pilot houses, the sterns and sidewheel housings were easily distinguished against the night sky.

I tied my horse and walked toward the bank of this semi-swamp for a close look. There were old snag boats, destroyed by the very snags they were seeking when disaster struck. There were ancient keelboats which had preceded the more resplendent steamboats. The remains of a showboat were also there, half submerged in the dark water and the mud. All of this bordered by a stand of thick cypress hung with garlands of gray Spanish moss.

I was searching for a riverboat bearing the name *Prince Maximilian* on its bow, or painted on its sidewheel housing.

To find it I had to move as close as possible to this graveyard of boats, risking a slip into the water if I got too close to the bank. One of the boats which seemed to have settled evenly in the water, lay out about twenty yards offshore. It looked to be the best preserved one of them all. I was unable to see any sign of a name painted on her, but I did consider her as the most likely prospect.

As I paused to try and figure out how I could manage to get aboard her, I saw a flicker of yellow light from her deck, as if someone had kept a lantern covered and only revealed the light momentarily to direct me.

So close to the shore that she was actually beached

there, lay one of the ancient keelboats with a wide, flat deck. I could easily step onto that. Perhaps if I crossed it I might find another deck to which I could transfer until I reached the boat where the signal light had shown so briefly.

I managed to get aboard the keelboat. The deck seemed sturdy and I began crossing it. Midway one of the boards all but crumpled under my weight, but as I'd been testing each step in anticipation of this, I was able to retain my balance and keep moving over the slanted deck.

At the other side of the deck I found about one half of a riverboat imbedded in the mud. To get aboard, I reached up for her deck rail and pulled myself up off the keelboat. I climbed over the rail, crossed that fairly narrow deck and crossed yet another ancient craft which led me to the lower deck of the ship which, I was now able to see, bore the name of *Prince Maximilian*.

I stood there in the darkness, listening and waiting. This was the right boat, I was on time, someone had shown a light. All I could do was wait to be approached or summoned.

Moments later my doubts began to grow, augmented by the silence and the gloom. If this was a trap, I doubted I'd manage to get away. I'd been warned and I'd heeded none of the stern suggestions that I not even leave the mansion. The lure of Marie's note had been too strong. Any potential murderer would have realized I'd never turn down a chance to find Marie.

If I met my death here, no one would find me for weeks. This desolate spot was rarely visited. I could scream with all my strength and not be heard. All the noise I could make would be unheeded, for there was no one within two or three miles of this point.

It was too marshy here, there were too many mosquitoes, as I was finding out. Often the river would leave its banks at this point and create massive flooding. The spot had been well chosen, if this was a trap.

I slapped at the pesky insects and finally I called

out. "Marie! Marie. . . . it's Jana Stewart." I waited for some sound to break the silence. "Marie . . . if you're here, please tell me so."

For some moments my words seemed to have been swallowed up by only silence. Then I heard a faint scraping sound. I saw again a flash of yellow light.

"Marie?" I asked. I might as well be talking to the wind.

The feeling of fear already growing within me blossomed into terror. Marie had sent for me. I was here. If she was able to come to me she would have. Either I'd been tricked and there was no Marie on the boat, or she'd been silenced and now it was my turn.

I began moving rapidly along the slanted deck, looking for a place where I could board the boat alongside. I skidded on something slippery, but managed to keep my balance. I became aware of the smell of some kind of oil. I had no idea where it came from, though it was quite possible I had slipped on this substance.

I reached the rail, grasped it and found that slippery too. This time I was able to raise my hand and smell the oil. There should be no oil aboard a ship abandoned for years, left to rot. Certainly there could be no use for oil here, unless . . . it was going to be used as fuel to set this boat and the whole graveyard afire.

I was about to consider leaping into the black water when the light reached me and I stood there, frozen in terror. Waiting for whoever held that lantern to emerge enough so that I might see who it was. There remained still a bare chance this was Marie. I had to stay and find out.

The light came closer. Whoever held it walked well behind it and the lantern was equipped with a reflector that threw all of the light forward so the person who held it was in shadow and all but unseen.

The light moved closer. I could hear the slow steps of the person who held it.

"Marie!" I screamed.

164

The light moved to one side, was raised high. I saw under it Walter's face, grimacing in either hatred or fear. He raised the lantern higher, whirled half about and threw it overboard. A second later I heard him coming for me. He skidded across the slippery deck. I could hear his breathing now as his lungs gasped in air.

"Walter!" I cried out. "Walter . . . no! Please, no . . .!"

His arms were around me. I was unable to move. I didn't know what was coming next, but it didn't seem to matter. I wilted in his grasp. I could fight no longer, not even if these were my last few seconds on earth.

Fifteen

Walter held me just as tightly, but he made no move to exert any further violence and I recovered my wits sufficiently that I managed to struggle. In the midst of this, I saw a ball of fire fly from shore to land on the deck where we stood. Instantly the oil-soaked, rotten wood began to blaze and the flames came toward us with an astonishing speed. At the same time other ancient, decaying craft also caught fire Many of them must have been soaked in highly inflammable oil.

Walter said nothing. He simply swept me into his arms, ran across the deck and threw me into the back-wash water, away from the burning craft. A few seconds elapsed and I saw him splash down close by me. We didn't swim toward the shore. We both knew someone would be there, possibly waiting to kill us if we managed to escape the flames. Instead we swam out in the direction of the river.

The water was stagnant, soupy and not easy to swim through, for it was laced with aquatic plants and tall grass that threatened to entangle me.

We reached the river water finally. It was calm, so we found no difficulty in swimming downstream for a con-siderable distance. Walter swam close to me.

"Head for the bank," he managed to wheeze loudly enough for me to hear.

I obeyed because I thought he knew this river better than I. The river bank went right down to the water. It was so shallow we straightened up and walked to dry land. Once there, we sought the protection of some brush where we sat down to regain our breaths. I began wringing out my dress, but I gave up when I decided it had absorbed about as much mud as water.

"Did you . . . get a letter . . . too . . .?" Walter was still breathless. His chest heaved as he sought to placate his aching lungs.

"Yes . . . from Marie," I said.

"Forgery," he said. "She never wrote it."

"I can believe it now," I said.

"Somebody was going to kill both of us. I got to the graveyard early, while it wasn't quite dark and I saw the oil. I didn't know what was going to happen, so I hid and waited. When you came along, I knew somebody was waiting for both of us to be there and then the fire would start."

"I thought you had set the trap for me," I said. My nerves were beginning to steady and I had stopped gasping for breath.

"But Jana, I had no reason to kill you."

"I thought you had. If I was dead, you could still wait for Marie to return."

"I don't think she's coming back."

"After what just happened, I don't think so either. Is it safe to go back to the plantation yet?"

"We have to find our horses. Maybe whoever did this is waiting for us. We'd better stay here awhile. It's not so bad. It's warm and the mosquitoes don't seem to be bothering us."

"We're likely so covered with mud they can't get at us," I managed to comment lightly, and it drew a brief chuckle from Walter. "I'm glad you didn't set that trap for me," I continued.

"All I tried to do was scare you away, so Papa couldn't insist I marry you."

"Who do you think did get us aboard that old boat and expected us to be burned to death?"

"Laverne," Walter said promptly.

"Why would he do such a thing? He's always been trying to help me."

"Because he's in love with you and he couldn't stand for you to marry anybody else, even me. I guess when Papa said we had to get married, Laverne decided if he couldn't have you, nobody would."

"Do you have any proof? Did you see him tonight?"

"No. Whoever it was kept out of sight. I'm just guessing, but who else is there?"

"I don't know. I suspected you because I knew you didn't want to marry me, and when I saw you on the boat you scared the daylights out of me."

"I'm sorry, Jana. I guess I'm pretty good at scaring you, but this time I didn't mean it. I wasn't sure who you were. For a second I thought Marie had come back to me."

"I wish she had, Walter. I'm sure now that you were really in love with her."

"I was. I still am. She's not worth it, but that's how it is. If she doesn't come back in the next few days, it'll be too late because you and I will be married."

"What a terrible thing," I said. "We're not in love. Not with one another. I'm in love with David Brennan, you're in love with Marie."

"I know. If I don't marry you he'll throw me out. I don't think I could even get a job I can handle. If you refuse to marry me, David's musical career is wrecked forever."

"After what just happened to us—being tricked and trapped that way, do you think your papa might relent?"

"Not him. It won't make the slightest difference to him, except maybe to speed everything up."

"We should do something about Laverne," I said.

"What? We can't prove anything. We didn't see him. The letter was written in a woman's hand, but he could have gotten someone to write it easily enough. And getting it mailed out of town was simple. I'm sure he's guilty, but we can't ask for help unless we can prove something."

It was a sultry night, but I was beginning to shiver

anyway from my wet clothing. I stood up and left the refuge we'd chosen, to look along the road nearby. Nothing moved.

"Let's go back and see if our horses are still there," I suggested.

"All right, but we've got to be careful. If it's Laverne, he might have seen us go into the water, figured we escaped, but we'd come back for the horses. He won't be waiting to shake our hands and congratulate us on not getting burned to death."

"I must change into something dry."

"I know. Maybe it's safe. If all those old boats are on fire, there must be quite a blaze. That'll draw a few people, and Laverne would know that and he'd get out of there. Wouldn't do for him to be caught around the scene."

Walter was right. We reached the area to find the fire had destroyed almost all of the boats. Those left were still smouldering. A dozen men had appeared.

"I left my horse well off the road to our right," Walter said. "I'll go get him. Meet me along the road, and don't let any of these people see you if you can help it."

I found myself not only obeying Walter's suggestions, but recognizing that they were sound. When he wanted to exert himself his intellect and judgment appeared to be very good. We'd not been friends prior to this attempt on our lives, but having faced death together, we were closer and I found myself beginning to like him.

I reached my horse, mounted and moved slowly along a trail which led to the road back to the plantation. I found Walter waiting for me around a bend in the road. He came out of the brush to intercept me and we rode side by side back to the plantation house.

"I didn't see anybody," Walter said.

"Nor I, except for the men watching the fire, and they didn't see me."

"Good."

We rode in silence then. I was shaken from my experience, but grateful that Walter was with me, otherwise I'd have been frantic. I recalled how terrified I'd been when I first saw his face in the lantern light, just before the firebrand came hurtling from shore. I'd made a mistake in believing him to be the person who'd tried to kill me. I realized how easy it was to make such an error when there was so little to go on.

I wasn't even sure that Laverne was guilty. I didn't intend to make any accusation. One mistake was enough. Yet it almost had to be Laverne. Perhaps he was in love with me. He'd always been so willing to help, he'd championed all of my causes and even defied Claude. But if he was that much in love with me, why would he seek to destroy me?

I'd given up any suspicions I'd had of Celina and Augusta. Odette might be capable of doing me harm, but I felt that what had happened was not the work of a woman, but a clever and ruthless man to whom my death was of extreme importance.

We reached the stables without being intercepted or seen. Walter helped me dismount. We stood quietly for a few minutes, listening and looking about.

"We've got to talk this over," Walter said. Tomorrow let's pretend we're going riding. I'll meet you at breakfast."

"I'll look forward to it," I said. "Thank you for what you did tonight. Just as David did during the sinking of the packet, you saved my life, in the same way. I'll be grateful as long as I live."

"Good night," he said. "If Laverne turns up in the morning before we ride, don't trust him."

I nodded and walked briskly back to the house. I prayed that no one locked the back door, which I'd left unlocked. It was still not secured, so I went in, used the back stairs and once in my room I hastily peeled off the muddy, damp riding habit. I then cleaned up as best I could. This was no hour to ask for bath water.

171

I didn't even want anyone to know I'd been out of the house.

My hair gave me the most trouble and I finally was compelled to wash it in cold water. In the morning I planned to ask Coleen to bring me water for a tub.

She looked in, bright and early, to see if there was anything I wanted and I put her to work at once. After a hot bath and another washing of my hair, I felt better. I sat in the early sunlight to dry my hair as much as possible before breakfast.

When I got there, Walter was already half through his meal. We were joined almost immediately by Claude.

"Well," he said, "you two are up early. That's unusual for you, Walter."

"Jana and I planned to go riding this morning," he said.

"Good. I'm very pleased. There's no reason you two can't get on well as man and wife. It would be all the better if this matter was settled on a friendly basis."

"That's what we thought," I said. "But I say again, Mr. Duncan, you will reinstate David at once."

"Of course. I'm going into the city today and move along the petition to declare Marie dead. I'll also pass a few hints to some of the French Opera Board of Directors that I may have been a trifle hasty in judging David, and perhaps we should reconsider. They'll all fall into line when I'm ready for them. Without my financial backing there wouldn't be an opera."

"Yes, Papa," Walter said. He laid down his napkin. "Ready, Jana?"

"Yes, Walter. It's a beautiful morning for a ride."

Claude nodded happily as we left the dining room. Walter and I strolled down to the stable where we waited until our horses were saddled. We rode out toward the pasture land where the stone fence was located, but halfway there, we turned away and rode away from the river until we came to the graveyard with its tombs. Walter pulled up.

172

"We've got to talk," he said, "but not here where we can be seen. Not far off either, because I want to watch the cemetery. I didn't sleep much all night thinking about this, and I want to find out how it impresses you."

"Then by all means let's find a place where we can talk," I said.

"Follow me," he said, and turned his horse sharply. We wound up tethering the horses out of sight. They'd been well fed and watered so there was no need for them to graze. We then walked back toward the cemetery until we located a dry, quiet spot beneath a cypress. Through the whiskers of gray moss we had a good view of the cemetery and we were not likely to be seen.

"Marie is dead," Walter said abruptly.

"Oh, Walter, don't tell me you found her . . .?"

"No . . . no, not that. But she'd have come back, or let me know where she was. All this time I've been fooling myself thinking she loved me and wouldn't stay away long. I guess she never loved me except for what Papa gave us. She wasn't a good woman, Jana. She cheated on me and I knew it. But I didn't know whom she was seeing. Now I'm sure it was Laverne."

I was astonished by that statement, but I quickly saw the sense to it. "Walter, we were looking for a motive that might make Laverne wish my death. We have one now. Don't you see?"

"Not exactly. I thought I was pretty good making up my mind it had to be him."

"It was good thinking. If Laverne was seeing Marie, he may have killed her. Did you think of that too?"

"First thing," he said morosely. "She's dead all right."

"If Laverne murdered her, then he would do anything to prevent your father from trying to get a legal judgment saying she was dead. No judge, no matter how much he was under your father's influence, would issue such an order without looking into it to some extent. Laverne must have reasons to believe any investigation might betray him. So—he would stop such an investigation by destroying the only reason for one. If I was killed, your father would likely drop his petition for Marie to be declared dead."

"We still have no proof," he insisted.

"Not so far," I admitted. Things were becoming clearer to me now, once we felt that Laverne must be guilty. "If he is worried that an investigation might turn up something, Marie's body must be hidden somewhere not far from the plantation."

Walter nodded. "That's why I wanted to hide here and watch the cemetery. If Laverne killed her, this is where he must have hidden the body. Like you just said, if she isn't close by, why does he worry so much he'd risk another murder to hide the first one? If he threw the body into the river and it got washed out to sea, or got snagged and hasn't been found so far, why would he worry? She's been gone a long time."

"A year," I said. "About that."

"Exactly one year ago today," he said and made it positive. "Here's the idea I got. Maybe it's all crazy like a lot of other ideas I get, but I think it's worth talking about."

"Walter, anything you say is worth listening to. You underestimate yourself."

"Maybe. I don't know. Anyway, if Laverne killed Marie, the best place he could hide her body is in one of those tombs."

"Of course it would be, but we can't go opening them all."

"No need to," he said mysteriously.

"I don't know, Walter. To open any of them would leave traces. They're cemented shut, some of them bricked over."

"That's right. It would be a lot of noisy work opening one. He sure couldn't have done it by day, and by night he'd wake everybody up. Unless. . . ."

"Unless what?" I asked, intrigued by this theory.

"Unless somebody else was buried that same day and

174

the cement was still soft, so all he had to do was get it out between the slab and the tomb. Then he could just put the slab back, add a little more fresh cement, which he could mix easily. There's always a lot of it in the storage sheds."

"Walter, all we have to do is look for a tomb dated a year ago today."

"It wouldn't be one of the family tombs," he said, "because nobody died for a long time. So it must be in that big one with all those niches. Some of them don't have the dates of birth and death. Folks who bury their dead there don't have enough money to more than scratch a name on the slab."

"Then how do we find it?" I asked.

"There's one thing all the folks on this plantation do without fail. Exactly one year after there's been a death in the family, the ones who are left will come to the cemetery and put flowers near the grave. It's like an unwritten law. So, if anybody was entombed one year ago today, some time today somebody will come with flowers. So we wait."

"And your papa has the idea you couldn't run this plantation," I said in open admiration.

"Sometimes I think I could, if I got the chance. But when you grow up with everybody thinking you're dumb, you never get a chance to show you're not. And pretty soon you begin thinking the same way. I thought of something else."

"I'm listening," I said.

"It wouldn't be so bad married to you. That is, if you could stand me."

"I'm sure we'd do fine, but Walter, you know it can never be."

"I know. Yes, I know for sure. I just thought I'd mention it. Believe me, just because we prove Laverne killed Marie won't make any difference to Papa. You'll see. He'll say we get married anyway."

"I hoped it might make a difference. His best friend killing his daughter-in-law."

"It won't. I know Papa."

"It seems to me," I said, "that we're getting a bit ahead of ourselves. We haven't found Marie yet. We don't know for certain if Laverne killed her. Even if we find her body, how do we prove he's guilty?"

"He must think we can, or he wouldn't try to kill you so Papa wouldn't reopen a search for Marie."

Walter lay back, shaded his eyes with his hat. "I'm still tired. Keep a sharp eye out, Jana. You see anybody, wake me up."

So it was left to me to sit quietly and keep the cemetery under constant observation. Just before noon, a woman entered the graveyard, but she wasn't carrying the traditional flowers. She held a trowel and with this she did some cleaning up around one of the family graves. Apparently she was assigned to care for it. After half an hour she departed.

Walter woke up shortly afterwards. We had little to say now. We were both intent on searching our minds for the final solution to this madness inspired by Claude's ambitions for a grandson.

It was mid-afternoon when a thin, bent man walked directly up to the big tomb. He was carrying a small bouquet of flowers. Each niche was provided with a hook and a metal urn. The man placed the flowers in one of these, bent his head for a few minutes and then walked away. We gave him twenty minutes before we hurried to the tomb. The flowers marked the location we wanted.

"I remember now," Walter said. "It was the funeral of a little girl. Maybe three or four years old. She died of the fever and was entombed here the same day." He examined the sealing cement. "Don't see any marks, but Laverne would have brushed them all away when he put in the fresh cement. I got to ride back and fetch some tools. You stay here. I won't be long."

He hurried to where his horse was tied and I heard

him ride off at top speed. I wondered if we were all wrong about this. Violating a grave, even that of a plantation worker, was no ordinary thing to do and if we were wrong, there'd have to be difficult explanations. Besides, if Marie's body was in there, we'd still lack the proof that Laverne was guilty, though I was now certain he must be.

Walter returned in less than half an hour, provided with a small pick, a sharp-ended lever and a hammer. He tied his horse to the cemetery fence. We saw no further need for secrecy.

"Papa is going to raise the roof if we're wrong," Walter told me, "but we've got to do this."

I said, "Walter, no matter how important this may be to me, I hope we don't find Marie's body in there. I hope she's alive and one day she'll come back to you."

He shook his head. "I got a feeling about this. She's in there."

He went to work, chiseling out the old cement until he had the slab loosened. He applied the lever, drew a long breath and pried open the tomb.

Stuffed inside, barely clearing the slab, was the body of a woman. It lay partly supported by the small casket of the child who had been interred a year ago.

Walter cried out and turned away quickly. He brought both hands to his face and then broke into a stumbling run until he disappeared in the growth of trees. I could still hear his wracking sobs.

I used his horse to return to the plantation where I summoned Claude. On the way back, with Claude riding grim faced beside me, I was trembling so that I had to hang on to the saddle.

Sixteen

Men were sent to the city to summon the authorities. When they arrived the grim task of removing the body took place. Not in my presence, for I retired abruptly to the house where I remained until Claude returned. So far, Walter hadn't appeared, but everyone was too busy to wonder where he might be.

"It was Laverne," Claude said grimly. "No question about it."

"How are you so sure?" I asked. "I believe he's guilty, but there's nothing. . . ."

"One must be certain before an accusation is made," Celina added.

She and Augusta had joined me to hear my story of the body stuffed into the niche.

"I cannot seem to reconcile myself to the fact that Laverne could be capable of such a thing," Augusta said. "He's such a gentleman."

"In this case," Claude said, "he was not. When he put Marie into the tomb, after strangling her, she wasn't quite dead. That he didn't know, or maybe he didn't care, but he should have. Marie found the strength to use the soft cement which oozed into the niche, to create Laverne's name on the coffin of the little girl in whose tomb she lay. It is there as the best possible evidence."

"Oh, the poor girl," Celina exclaimed.

"She didn't deserve that," Claude said. "Where's Walter?"

No one had seen him. Claude jumped to his feet. "The fool may be on his way to New Orleans to find Laverne and kill him. Not that I blame him, but that will only mean more trouble. I've got to head him off if I can . . ."

Claude hadn't even reached the stable for a horse when we saw Walter ride up slowly, bent over the saddle like a man too ill to ride. Claude came running back in time to hold the horse steady while Walter all but fell out of the saddle. He looked about. He must have seen us gathered there, but he showed no sign of recognizing any of us.

He spoke in a monotone. "Laverne is dead."

"Walter, that was wrong, but I'll stand by you," Claude said. "You had reason enough. . . ."

"I didn't kill him. I was pounding on his door when he shot himself."

Celina and Augusta sobbed as they walked slowly back to the house. Walter, his arm held by Claude, followed them and I came up at the rear.

I was sick at heart because of the ending of this awful affair. Of course everything was clear now. Laverne had been responsible for all the attacks on me. Maybe, beside trying to keep the body of Marie hidden, he had been in love with me. I didn't know, but the very thought of it made me shudder.

Walter went to bed with a sedative. So did Augusta. Odette prepared supper, but nobody was in a mood to enjoy food, though we went to the table and picked at it.

"Walter shouldn't grieve this way," Claude said. "She wasn't worth that."

"She's dead. Let the poor girl have her peace," Celina urged. "I'm only glad that Walter didn't kill Laverne. That I wouldn't have been able to bear. To think all this happened under our very eyes and we had no inkling of it."

"I certainly never believed Laverne capable of such a thing," Claude said. "It proves we never know what our neighbors are up to. Well, it's over now."

"Is it?" I asked quietly.

180

Claude knew what I meant. Celina looked at me questioningly.

"There is no longer any need to obtain a court order declaring Marie dead," Claude said. "That simplifies things."

"You haven't changed your mind?" I asked.

He seemed surprised. "Why should I, Jana? What has this to do with my plans? With my grandson?"

"Stop it," Celina said sharply. "This is not the time to speak of such matters."

"Jana brought it up, I didn't. She wanted an answer. I gave it to her. The deaths of Marie and Laverne are in no way connected with my wedding plans for Jana and Walter. In fact, we can hold the wedding much sooner. Nobody is going to think it strange that Walter marry so soon after Marie's body was found."

"It's indecent," Celina said, and arose from the table.

"Marie never did deserve Walter's sorrow or tears," Claude said. "Laverne tricked all of us, even planned to kill Jana. Why should we grieve for him? There's nothing to grieve about. Let the wedding take place quickly."

"Not," I said, "until after David returns and I can explain to him what has happened."

"I agree to that, Jana. But tell him more than what happened during his absence. Tell him what is going to happen. He'll get over it. The night after he conducts the première he'll know it was worth it. So will you. Now I've had my say. There's work to be done in the library. Good evening, Celina, my dear. Good evening, Jana."

Celina said, "You won't be able to change his mind, my dear."

"I know. I'll tell David. It will be the most difficult thing I ever did in my life, but I have given my word. David must have his chance."

"He will know one thing for certain," Celina observed. "That you love him with all your heart. I doubt I'd be able to do what you are doing. I even question the wisdom of it, but I do see your point. I promise that if you marry Walter, I shall see to it that your life is made as pleasant as possible. You changed my life, now it will be my turn to help you."

I could find no comment, so I merely thanked her and went to my rooms. Tomorrow David would return from the sad journey I'd sent him on. Possibly the day after I would marry Walter. My world was coming to an end.

The fact that my life was no longer in danger brought a sense of relief, but there was no joy in it. David would be aboard a packet that would dock late in the morning. I'd have to be there with a welcome that would destroy every hope we ever had. I knew how hard he'd argue that the cost of his success was too much, but I had given my word and Claude could still destroy David. Without that threat over my head, I should have defied Claude, even now, after I'd told him I'd go through with the demands he made of me. A promise obtained under such duress would have little moral meaning to me.

I dressed carefully in the morning, though I didn't feel much like it. I had a buggy brought around and after a breakfast I ate little of, I was ready to proceed to New Orleans and meet David.

"It will prove to be best for both of you," Claude said. "After a time there will be no regrets. Walter is not a monster, after all."

"Walter," I said, "is a fine young man and he deserves to select his own wife."

"He made a sorry business of it the first time, Jana. I don't agree with you. Besides, as I often stated, it's your blood line I want merged with my family."

"What of your promise to reinstate David?"

"There is to be a full meeting of the Board of Directors this afternoon. Before the day is out David shall have his contract. Two days later he will conduct the première, this time successfully."

"He would have been successful the first time, had it not been for you," I said bitterly. "I will never forgive you for what you did."

182

"In time you will. I'm a successful man, Jana, and to reach that status in life you have to be tough and uncompromising. You have to get what you go after without fail. That holds true in business and in a man's personal life. I may not enjoy some of the things I am compelled to do, but when they must be done my conscience remains clear."

I didn't answer him. I climbed aboard the buggy and started on the saddest journey of my life.

As the packet docked and the deck hands shouted for the gangplank to be lowered, I saw David at the rail, searching the crowd on the dock for me. I waved. He raised both hands and waved back. He was one of the first off the boat and he embraced and kissed me with a fervor I returned. For the last time, I thought.

"My news will have to wait," he said. "I heard about Laverne and Marie. Word went up the river last night and I was told about it at a refueling stop we made. I want to know the details, but above all I'm delighted that he was found out in time. Now you're no longer in danger."

"It was an awful ending to a horrible affair," I said. "David, please drive the buggy to some quiet place, not in the city. There's so much for us to talk about."

He looked at me sharply. "What's wrong? You look as if you've been crying. It's Claude, isn't it?"

"First, a quiet place," I said.

He urged the horse into a fast run and drove out of the city to a turnoff in the road where he pulled up beside the river. He turned to me and I told him about the attack on me and Walter at the steamboat graveyard, how we reasoned where Marie's body must be and how Marie, in her dying moments, had accused Laverne of her murder.

"I'm glad Walter didn't kill Laverne," I said. "I'm afraid it would have been something he'd find difficult to live with. Walter is not the same man. He's changed for the better and that has made me happy."

"Why?" David asked quickly. I was sure he knew what was coming.

"Because I'm going to marry him."

David gave me a wide smile and a hard shake of his head. "You're going to marry me. Walter may have turned into a fine man, but you're not going to be his wife."

"I've given my word."

"To Claude?"

"Yes. This afternoon he goes before the Board of Directors of the French Opera and you will be reinstated, with a firm contract and at a higher salary than already agreed upon."

"Will Claude also reveal that he was responsible for what happened the night of the première?"

"How can you ask that of a man like Claude?"

"My darling Jana, with a man like Claude, you don't ask. You tell the Board what he did. I can prove it."

"To what purpose beyond destroying any chance you will have in New Orleans, or the entire world for that matter? You know Claude's influence reaches far."

"I will not let you do this," he said.

"It's all but done. Soon Walter and I will be married. Claude doesn't even have to get a court order declaring Marie dead now."

"What about Walter? Is he in love with you?"

"No, he is not, and he never will be. I doubt he'll ever get over Marie, no matter how tragic the ending of his marriage to her turned out to be."

"You are willing to marry a man you don't love, bear his children, because Claude demands it of you? All to insure my success as a conductor?"

"Of course," I said. "I love you, David. Sometimes love demands sacrifices. I will not allow you to be professionally ruined, even if it means I lose you."

He seemed almost annoyingly sure of himself. I thought he was trying to cheer me up. Or, perhaps, insist we be married at once in defiance of Claude.

"Will you attend the meeting of the Board of Directors this afternoon?" he asked.

"If that is your wish."

"Good. Because I want you there. Now all of this can be settled later. There is still my mission to explain. I found no trace of your father and mother. I dove into the water at the scene of the wreck many times. I'm sorry."

"Now I know." I pressed my face against his shoulder and wept for a short time. I'd expected no more than this, but even so, it brought back all the sorrow I'd felt immediately after the tragedy. David's arms were about me. In them I found the strength to face up to it all, but it was a fresh and awful disappointment to know that I could never draw upon his strength again.

"I suggest," he said, "that we cheer up to some extent. Let's have dinner at the hotel and then attend the meeting."

I dried my tears. "As you wish, David. Promise me one thing."

"I know what you're going to ask. I'm not to make any accusation against Claude."

"Is that too much to ask of you?"

"No, certainly not."

"And swear that you will accept the position they offer you."

"You have my word. Now I wish a promise from you."

"Oh, David, all I want is to get this over with. If it goes on much longer, I'll go out of my mind. I'm here with you, held in your arms, knowing it's for the last time. Please take me to the hotel where there are a lot of people so I can get hold of myself."

"I ask a promise," he insisted.

"Whatever it is, yes. I'll do anything you say, except refuse to marry Walter."

"This business of my being rehired is based upon the fact that the Board of Directors cannot refuse anything Claude wants, because without his financial help, the

French Opera will not be able to function. Is that true?"

"Only too true."

"If Claude's backing was no longer required, would the Board then go about their business and disregard whatever he commands?"

"No doubt. What are you getting at?"

"If we defeat Claude's efforts to hold that club over our heads, will you marry me tomorrow?"

"I'd marry you this instant. What is it, darling? What's happened?"

"A rather unusual thing. Up to now, Claude held our happiness in the hollow of his hand. Do as he says and we'd find an end to our troubles. Defy him and he'd close that hand and crush us. Well, our happiness is no longer in his hands."

"What are you talking about?" My hopes were beginning to rise, though there was nothing to base that upon except David's confidence.

"Never mind dinner. Let's go over to the French Opera and wait for the meeting to begin. I want to soak in some of the glory of that opera house because I'm going to make it even more famous and successful. I know I can."

"I wish you'd tell me. . . ."

He cut me off by kissing me. "With you beside me, I can do anything. I'll have but one more question to ask and that won't be until the meeting is on."

The interior of the opera house was cool and comfortable. We walked down the center aisle with David humming one melodious section of the overture. We stood beside the front row and looked into the pit, at the stand where he'd direct. I could not only see how excited he was, but some of the excitement—and hope—found its way into my heart. I'd tried a dozen times to make him tell me what secret he held, but he gleefully refused and I had to be content.

In the Green Room, where patrons gathered before the performances and during intermissions, there had been set up a table and chairs for the meeting. We were early, but the time passed quickly as we went through the theatre and David talked of other operas he wished to direct here.

Presently, some of the board members appeared. They were pleasant to David, but somewhat cool. As if they didn't know which way Claude was going to insist they jump. Finally they were all present and Claude came marching in. He went directly up to us and wrung David's hand as if he hadn't seen him in weeks and welcomed him back as warmly as possible. Then Claude assumed his place at the head of the table.

"I am not a man to readily admit I've been wrong," he said. "In this case I was. By a precipitate judgment I decided David Brennan did not have the ability or talent to take over the most important role of conductor. This was on the face of a rather sorry performance which I blamed on him. Wrongfully, I now admit. He was entirely blameless, so I now ask that we reconsider the contract we offered him, draw up a new one at an increased length of service—for we must not let him get away from us—and at a better salary which will improve with time. If there are any questions, may I have them now before we vote?"

There were no questions, only happy agreement with his statement. It was so evident that all of them wanted David to direct. I felt a glow of pride and in that I would find some measure of solace when I would no longer see him except from the audience.

David arose. "May I be heard, gentlemen?"

"Certainly," Claude said in his most expansive manner.

David bent down to whisper. "Darling, if it was within your ability to change this situation and deliver the management of this opera house into the hands of the Board of Directors and away from Claude's influence, would you do this?"

"Why . . . yes," I said vaguely, because I didn't quite know what he was talking about.

"Even at considerable cost?"

187

"David, what are you trying to tell me?"

"Would the cost be of little concern?"

"Of course."

"And will you place yourself and everything you have into my keeping for the time being, so that I may exert my own judgment in handling this matter?"

"In one more moment I shall refuse anything you ask unless you tell me what this is all about."

"In that case," he said, "I'd better not say anything more to you, my dear." He walked to the head of the table and stood beside Claude's chair.

"Gentlemen," he said, "I appreciate your confidence in me and I'll do my utmost to warrant it. There is only one thing I dislike and that is Claude Duncan's absolute rule of this theatre because he contributes enough to keep it solvent. Under these circumstances, under Claude Duncan's rule, I will not accept any contract."

I gasped aloud. I hadn't expected this. The members of the Board seemed stunned and Claude was scowling heavily.

David went on. "However, I shall be delighted to accept if Mr. Duncan's absolute rule over this theatre and this Board of Directors is done away with. Now be patient. I know what all of you are thinking. The financial backing of this theatre will from now on come from another source. Miss Jana Stewart directs me to announce that she will finance the theatre from here on."

He unbuttoned his coat, unbuckled a heavy, wide belt which he'd worn outside his shirt, though I'd not noticed it. He placed this on the table.

"In this money belt, gentlemen, is Miss Stewart's personal wealth. Her father was on his way to New Orleans to set up in business and he carried with him a small fortune. In this belt is sufficient for all your purposes, and a great deal more besides. You will ask why she did not come forward before. Her father and mother were killed in the destruction of a packet some weeks ago, as you all no doubt remember. It seems that her

188

ather had returned to his stateroom and removed this money belt from his person and placed it in a bureau drawer. A sturdy, built-in drawer which survived the explosion and the fire. I found it there and I am now returning it to Miss Stewart. She will now take her place at the head of this table, as the principal backer of the theatre. Mr. Duncan, do you mind?"

Claude arose slowly. His face had turned a deep red as David spoke, but that faded rapidly. When I approached the table he took both my hands in his.

"I am not accustomed to defeat, my dear, but I acknowledge that you and your young man have won. Whatever promises you made to me do not have to be fulfilled. I only ask that you will remain my good friend and allow me in some manner to make up for the distress I no doubt caused you."

I said, "I never did think you were as bad as you growled, Mr. Duncan."

He chuckled, shook David's hand, took a chair down the length of the table and the business of the day was begun and finally concluded with me still in a somewhat dazed condition.

Claude approached David and me again. "Good luck," he said. "I'd be proud if you'd be married at my home. In fact, I insist upon it, and I shall invite all of the most important people in New Orleans to attend. Will you do this for me?"

"Yes," I said. "Gladly."

"Something tells me," David said, "that there's more than simple generosity here, Mr. Duncan."

"I thought you'd be hard to deceive, David. I'll have every marriageable girl in the city at your wedding. I'll have Walter there as well. I'm not licked yet."

He walked away, chuckling to himself. David laughed too.

"He'll never change."

"Now that I'm safe, I don't think I want him to," I said. We left the Green Room and found ourselves among

189

the stalls. We sat down in a center one and looked at the stage below us.

"I'm sorry I had to surprise you," David said, "but I was afraid if Claude found out what I planned he'd take steps to stop me. As I told the Board of Directors, I found the money belt. On my way to the wreck, I thought how we could change things if your father's money were found. I spent a day diving for it. Now you're the most important patroness of this opera house. I am only the conductor. I shall from here on take my orders from you."

"Marry me soon," I said. "That's the only order I will give you now or ever."

We sat there for a long, long time.